"Men have kind of taken a back seat in my life, you know?"

He got that. In a lot of ways, he was the same—minus the big family and the sister who was also a best friend. He had loved his sister, but once they grew up, they'd chosen different paths. Until Megan and Kevin went down in that plane, his life had centered on Stryker Marine.

"What about you?" she asked. "Anyone special?"

He'd figured that was coming. Still, he hesitated, though he knew it would be better just to put it right out there. Rip the bandage off, so to speak.

"Trying to decide how much to say?" she teased.

He went ahead and busted himself. "You got me."

Her big eyes had grown wary. "So there is someone, then?"

"No—but I was engaged until recently."

She blinked. Probably not a good sign. "How recently?"

"We broke up last Friday."

* * *

THE BRAVOS OF VALENTINE BAY: They're finding love—and having babies!—in the Pacific Northwest

Dear Reader,

It's a bittersweet Christmas for Harper Bravo—the last Christmas she'll be living in Valentine Bay, Oregon. Yes, she loves her hometown and her large family. But it's time for a new start in the big city. In February, she's moving to Seattle, where she will be changing careers.

For Portland-based shipping magnate Lincoln Stryker, it's a Christmas like no other. This year, Linc lost a sister—and became guardian and stand-in dad to her two beautiful children. He wants to give five-year-old Jayden and two-year-old Maya the perfect Christmas in the Stryker family cottage on the edge of the Pacific in Valentine Bay, just him and the kids sharing the holidays the way he and his sister did way back when. There's only one little problem. Linc might possibly have taken on more than he can deliver.

But then he meets the gorgeous woman next door. Harper is not only down-to-earth and a lot of fun, she's great with the kids. He offers her a job as temporary nanny. Harper, who is saving money for her big move, says yes.

Neither of them wants to mess with the program. But the attraction between them is sizzling hot. They shouldn't...and they promise each other they won't. But after all, it's Christmastime. And in the magic of the season, how can it possibly be a bad idea to follow where their hearts lead them?

I hope Harper and Linc's story warms your heart, makes you laugh and maybe has you wiping away a tear or two.

Merry Christmas, happy Hanukkah and a glorious Kwanzaa to one and all,

Christine

A Temporary Christmas Arrangement

CHRISTINE RIMMER

HARLEQUIN
SPECIAL
EDITION

HARLEQUIN®
SPECIAL EDITION™

ISBN-13: 978-1-335-89495-3

A Temporary Christmas Arrangement

Copyright © 2020 by Christine Rimmer

This edition published by arrangement with Harlequin Books S.A.

For questions and comments about the quality of this book, please contact us at CustomerService@Harlequin.com.

Harlequin Enterprises ULC
22 Adelaide St. West, 40th Floor
Toronto, Ontario M5H 4E3, Canada
www.Harlequin.com

Printed in U.S.A.

Christine Rimmer came to her profession the long way around. She tried everything from acting to teaching to telephone sales. Now she's finally found work that suits her perfectly. She insists she never had a problem keeping a job—she was merely gaining "life experience" for her future as a novelist. Christine lives with her family in Oregon. Visit her at christinerimmer.com.

Visit the Author Profile page
at Harlequin.com for more titles.

For MSR, always.

Chapter One

The drive from Portland to Valentine Bay started out just as Lincoln Stryker had been certain it would. Both kids seemed happy. Linc had everything under control.

A glance in the rearview mirror revealed five-year-old Jayden in the car seat directly behind Linc. The boy gazed dreamily out the window.

Jayden was a talker. He might be lazily watching the world go by, but he didn't do it silently. Not Jayden. He chattered nonstop. "Uncle Linc, I hope the nice ladies next door are home. Did you meet the nice ladies?"

Had he? Linc had no clue. Probably not. "At the cottage, you mean?"

"Yes. They are Harper and Hailey and I like them a lot."

"I don't think I've met them." Linc hadn't been to his family's seaside cottage in more than a decade. His hazy, fond memories of the place didn't include the neighbors.

And as it turned out, Jayden didn't care if Linc knew the "nice ladies" or not. The little boy babbled on, "Harper and Hailey are sisters and they are so much fun. I was only four last Christmas, but I 'member. I 'member everything. I 'member they came over to play and they helped me make a snowman—and that 'minds me. There should be snow, Uncle Linc. There should be snow, and Harper and Hailey can help me make a snowman. Will you help, too?"

Linc took his eyes off the road long enough to cast a quick look over his right shoulder at two-year-old Maya in the other car seat. She was already asleep, her plush stuffed pig, Pebble, clutched in her chubby little arms.

"Uncle Linc, will you help me make my snowman?" Jayden asked more insistently.

Linc faced the road again, caught Jayden's eye in the rearview and winked at him. "Absolutely, I will."

"Good. And don't forget the Christmas tree…"

"I won't."

"I 'member last year we had a tall one."

Linc felt a sharp pang of sadness. "I'm sure you

did." Megan—Jayden's mom and Linc's only sibling—had always required a real tree, a tall one.

"I want one like that this year, too, Uncle Linc."

"A tall one, it is." Megan Hollister had loved Christmas. For all her too-short life, she'd insisted that the holidays should be spent at the Stryker family cottage on the coast.

"We have to put on all the lights," Jayden said. "All the lights and the red shiny balls and the little toy soldiers and the angel on the very top…"

Linc pushed his sadness aside and focused on the wide, gently curving road ahead as Jayden happily chattered away. The kid was intrepid in the best sense of the word. Nothing got him down.

And Linc would do everything in his power to make sure that Jayden—and Maya, too—had a good Christmas this year, the kind of Christmas Megan would have given them if she were still here. It was going to be Linc and his niece and nephew, from Thanksgiving through New Year's. Family only, the way Megan would have wanted it.

The kids' grandma Jean had tried to convince Linc that he would need a nanny at the cottage, especially if he hoped to work remotely. Jean Hollister was a wonderful woman. Jayden and Maya adored her—rightfully so. But Jean didn't know everything.

Linc and Jayden and Maya would manage just fine. No nanny required until after Christmas, when they returned to Portland and Linc went back to the office full-time.

"Uncle Linc, I'm hungry…"

"You think maybe you can hold on until we get to the cottage?"

"I'll try…" Jayden lasted exactly three minutes. "Uncle Linc, my tummy is *growling*…"

They were just passing Hillsboro, so there were still plenty of fast-food places with drive-throughs. Linc pulled into the next one.

As he rolled down the window to put in Jayden's order, Maya jolted awake with a startled little whimper. She fussed as they moved on to the pickup window, where Jayden's snack waited.

A few minutes later, they rolled out onto the road again. Maya had not stopped fussing. But with any luck, she would be lulled back to sleep by the ride.

Ten minutes later, Maya's whines had turned to all-out wails. Linc pulled off at the next opportunity and checked her diaper. It was wet, so he changed it.

Jayden waited until they were back on the road to mention that he really, really had to pee.

It went on like that. One thing after another, a classic car-ride-with-the-kids experience. What with stopping to offer comfort to whichever child was upset, change a loaded diaper, get Jayden another snack and then, soon after, yet another potty break, the hour-and-a-half drive took almost twice that long.

When Linc finally pulled the Range Rover in at the cottage on the wooded bluffs above the ocean in Valentine Bay, it was after three and the shadows had grown longer. It would be dark by five.

And Maya had started crying again.

Jayden just kept on talking. "We're here! I want to see the nice ladies. I want to go get the Christmas tree…"

"One thing at a time, Jayden." In the phone holder, Linc's cell lit up. Again. He let it go to voice mail. Already, he'd ignored several calls from the office, where they damn well ought to be able to get through one day without him.

He needed to unload the car, get the kids inside; settle them down a little; turn on the water, the power and the heat; and put something together for dinner—and okay, fine. Maybe he should have listened to Jean and considered bringing help.

At the very least, he could have called the property manager to get the water running, the lights on and the place warmed up.

But he hadn't. Because it was tradition, after all. The Strykers might be one of the wealthiest families in Oregon, a fortune built on four generations of running Stryker Marine Transport coupled with smart investment strategies, but when Christmastime came around, having money running out their ears didn't matter.

At the cottage, Linc's family did for themselves. His happiest childhood memories were in Valentine Bay. At the cottage, he and Megan had almost felt like they belonged to a regular family, the kind where the mom and dad actually cared about each other and spent time with their kids.

And damn it, he could do this.

He *would* do this.

He just needed to take it one step at a time.

First up: try to settle the wailing Maya down a little.

Jayden announced, "I'm gonna get out and—"

"Jayden."

"What, Uncle Linc?"

"I need you to stay in your car seat for a few minutes. Will you do that for me?"

Jayden wrinkled his nose, like the idea of staying put smelled bad. "There's french fries under my butt."

"We'll deal with that, I promise. For right now, though, just sit tight."

Maya had sailed past crying and straight on to wailing. "Unc Winc!" she screamed, and threw her beloved stuffed pig on the floor.

"She's hurting my ears!" whined Jayden. Ever resourceful, he stuck his fingers in them. "There." He let out a long sigh. "That's better."

Linc flashed the boy a big thumbs-up, after which he climbed from the car, ran around to Maya's door and extricated the unhappy toddler from her seat. "Here we go, sweetheart." He hoisted her into his arms.

She grabbed him around the neck and screamed all the louder, burying her sweaty little face in the crook of his shoulder, smearing him with snot and unhappy tears.

He stroked her dark, baby-fine curls and soothed, "Shh, now. It's okay…"

Pulling open the front passenger door, Linc laid her on the seat and somehow managed, through her layers of winter clothing, to get two fingers down the back of her diaper. It was a bold and dangerous move, but it turned out all right. She hadn't soiled her diaper, which meant her two-year-old molars were probably acting up again.

Maya confirmed the problem, pressing small fingers to her jaw. "Hurt, Unc Winc." She needed a cold washcloth to chew on, but he couldn't give her one until they were inside the cottage and he'd turned on the water. Jean had taught him to stick his fingers in her mouth and massage the area. But he hated to do that without washing his hands first.

"I'll help," announced Jayden, and snapped himself out of his car seat before Linc could order him to stay put.

Which was okay, come to think of it. "You're the best, Jayden. Get that blue chew thing out of the front of her diaper bag…" It was soft silicone and shaped to fit in the back of her mouth.

Jayden crouched in the footwell to dig around in the bag. "Got it!" Beaming proudly, he handed the teething toy over the seat to Linc.

"Great job—now, stay close," Linc warned.

When left to his own devices, Jayden sometimes went off "adventuring."

"I will, Uncle Linc…"

"Thanks." Linc gave the screaming little one her chew toy. She knew what to do, sticking it into her mouth with a sad little moan, holding the soft handle while chewing the business end into the spot she needed it, all the way in back. The silence that followed was golden. "Better?" he asked.

Her expression relaxed and she made a soft, contented sound as she worked the toy inside her mouth.

He glanced over the seat at Jayden again. "Can you hand me Maya's baby sling?"

"Yep." The little boy dug out the sling and passed it to Linc.

Linc thanked him enthusiastically and then got down to the business of putting Maya into the sling, all nice and cozy against his chest. She was still small enough to carry that way—though she wouldn't be for long. He spoke to her softly as she chewed on the blue toy and stared up at him with so much trust in those big brown eyes.

Megan's eyes…

The sadness dragged at him again. He refused to surrender to it. Megan and Kevin were gone. But they lived on through Maya and Jayden—and Linc would do whatever it took to give his niece and nephew a happy childhood and a decent start in life.

Maya, attached to the front of him now, chewed

away on her teething toy and reached up her free hand to gently pat his cheek.

His heart suddenly too big for his chest, he smiled down at her. "Okay, then, sweetheart. Let's go on into the…"

Was it suddenly much too quiet?

He glanced into the back seat, where Jayden's door gaped wide-open. The boy was no longer crouched in the footwell and, except for a few smashed fries, his car seat sat empty. "Jayden?"

No answer.

"Jayden!"

Silence.

Maya stared up at him, eyes wide as saucers. She made a tiny, anxious sound. "It's okay," he soothed her, rubbing her back as he turned in a circle, his gaze probing the shadows between the giant Douglas firs that loomed all around. "Jayden!"

Again, no answer. Linc's heart pounded the walls of his chest and his pulse roared in his ears.

He'd only taken his attention off the kid for a minute or two, tops. And yet somehow, in that those minutes, he'd vanished.

"Jayden?"

Still no answer. Linc tamped down a hard spurt of adrenaline-boosted terror. No reason to lose it yet. Jayden couldn't have gone far.

In the rambling family-owned cottage she used to share with her sister, Harper Bravo stared into the wide-open fridge and tried to decide what to have for dinner. Nothing looked good. She was just about to check the freezer when the doorbell rang.

Company. Her mood brightened. Harper had yet to become accustomed to living alone. She would love a little company, even old Angus McTerly, who lived two cottages south and had no doubt lost track of his wandering dog, Mitsy.

But it wasn't Angus. She pulled the door wide and found little Jayden Hollister, whom she hadn't seen since last Christmas, waiting on the step.

"Hi, Harper." He threw his arms wide and beamed up at her from under the blue hood of his down jacket. "It's me!"

"Jayden. What a surprise."

"Is Hailey here, too?"

"Um, not right now." The boy, who'd grown a good three inches since the last time she'd seen him, appeared to be on his own. Whoever was supposed to be watching him probably wondered where he'd gotten off to. "Jayden, are you all by yourself?"

He tipped his head to the side and looked up at her through a fringe of thick, dark eyelashes. "Not ezackly…" And he launched into a chatty little monologue about his uncle and his sister and how they were all in the car for "a reeeely long time." From there, he segued into how he hoped it would snow and there could be a snowman like last year. "And we will be here all the way to New Year's Day, Harper, so can I be in the Christmas show again and you can make me an elf suit like you did before?" Harper and her sister Hailey put on several community events a year at the Valentine Bay Theatre downtown—and Jayden had quite the memory for a five-year-old.

"Did you say your uncle is here with you?"

"Yes!"

"Let me check with him about the Christmas show, okay?"

"Okay!"

She stuck her phone in her pocket and grabbed her old wool Pendleton from the hook by the door. When she wiggled her fingers at him, Jayden took her hand. "Tell you what. Let's go on back to your cottage, shall we? Your uncle is probably wondering where you are."

"All right, let's go!" Jayden skipped along beside her as they took the narrow, tree-lined path that led to the next cottage north of hers.

Halfway there, a handsome and harried-looking man appeared from around the next bend. He had a second child strapped to his chest in a baby sling— undoubtedly Maya, who was about two years old now. And the hot guy? The uncle in question, the one who took guardianship of the children when their parents had died so tragically last January.

Like most people in town, Harper had read about the plane crash in the news. Such a heartbreaking story, and it must be so hard for the family—the two innocent kids, especially. But for the uncle, as well.

He'd lost his sister and his brother-in-law. Harper understood that kind of loss from firsthand experience.

"Jayden!" The uncle sounded as frantic as he looked. "There you are. You scared me to death." The little girl in the baby sling started fussing, and Jayden, alarmed at the uncle's wild-eyed expression, stopped stock-still on the path.

"Hi, I'm Harper." She spoke in a cheerful, non-threatening tone and plastered a big smile on her face, hoping the uncle would take the hint, lower his voice and stop scaring the kids. "Jayden and I are friends," she said brightly. "We know each other from last Christmas. Are you staying at the Stryker cottage?"

The uncle turned his angry glare on her. "Where else would we be?"

Still in her child-soothing voice, she suggested softly, "You need to smile. Because a smile would be so much less scary than your face right now."

Linc finally got what the woman with Jayden was trying to tell him. "Uh, right." Bouncing Maya gently to calm her down, he drew a deep breath and rearranged his expression to something he hoped came off as not quite so freaked. "I apologize for the scariness. I was worried…"

"I completely understand." The woman—Harper?—softened her smile. Linc found himself thinking how pretty she was, with long, thick blond hair and enormous pale blue eyes in a heart-shaped face.

He introduced himself. "I'm Linc Stryker, the kids' uncle and guardian."

"Great to meet you, Linc." She cast a downward glance at the wide-eyed Jayden and then arched an eyebrow at Linc.

He took her meaning and spoke gently to the little boy. "Jayden, I'm sorry for using such a loud voice. But remember, no adventuring without an adult."

Jayden gave him a slow and very serious nod. "I'm sorry, too, Uncle Linc. I shouldn't have left like that, and I won't do it again—and I wasn't adventuring, not really. I just wanted to say hi to Harper and Hailey."

"I get it. But leaving without telling me where you're going is not okay."

"I know, Uncle Linc. I *promise* I won't do that again."

"Excellent."

Right then, Maya whined, "Unc Winc, I hungwy!"

He dropped a kiss on the top of her curly head. "Okay. Let's see what we can do about that." He held out his hand for Jayden, who let go of Harper to take it. "Thank you," he said to the blonde.

"Anytime." Her soft mouth bloomed in a radiant smile as he turned to take the kids back the way they'd come.

Harper felt weirdly stunned.

The uncle was way too attractive, tall and broad shouldered with caramel-brown eyes and full lips and a sculpted jaw dusted with just the right amount of scruff—and where were her manners?

Linc Stryker could clearly use a hand.

"Wait." When he paused and glanced back at her, she offered, "Let me help. What can I do?"

Linc turned fully around again and grinned at her, a slow grin that caused the muscles in her belly to tighten and warmth to flare across her skin. "I've been trying really hard to pretend that I've got this."

"Pretend? No way. It's obvious to me that you know what you're doing."

He scoffed. "If you say so."

"I do. Now and then, though, you need to let a neighbor give you a hand."

"You're sure?"

"Honestly, I'm happy to help."

"Hungwy, hungwy, hungwy," chanted the little one in the baby sling, reaching up to capture Linc's face between her hands.

He caught the teething toy she'd dropped and bent to whisper something to her. When he glanced up, he aimed that sexy smile at Harper again. "Help would be wonderful."

"So, what can I do?"

"I hate to ask…"

"Just tell me."

"Well, if you would maybe come on back to the cottage with us? I would owe you big-time if you could keep an eye on the kids until I can unpack the car and get the power and the heat turned on…"

* * *

The Strykers' charming, gray-shingled two-story vacation house was a cottage in name only. Harper guesstimated the size at around four thousand square feet, with a beautiful, modern kitchen and lots of windows offering forest and ocean views.

"It's been updated since last year, hasn't it?" she asked, when they stood in the kitchen—still wearing their coats because the heat wasn't on yet. "I remember seeing workmen here, in July and August…"

Linc gave Maya back her teething toy. "I hired a contractor last summer to upgrade the kitchen and bathrooms. Then in September, I arranged for a decorator to come in. She had all the rooms painted and changed out the furniture." His warm brown eyes looked shadowed suddenly. Harper had a sense he was thinking of the sister he'd lost. "I wanted to bring the kids here for the holidays and the place needed an upgrade or two."

"It's beautiful," she said.

"I like it!" declared Jayden.

Linc seemed pleased. He ruffled the boy's hair. "I'm glad to hear it meets with your approval." He glanced down at the little girl attached to his chest and then up at Harper. "If you'll take Maya, I'll get busy unloading the car."

Harper helped him unhook the sling. When he handed the little one over, Maya didn't protest, just reached out her arms and let Harper gather her in, taking the blue teething toy out of her mouth long enough to remark, "I hungwy. Now."

"We'll fill up that tummy. Promise." Harper brushed a kiss on her plump cheek.

Linc brought in the food first—what there was of it. "It's not much," he confessed sheepishly. "I had this idea I would just take the kids out with me to get everything we needed right here in town." He set the two bags of groceries on the white marble countertop.

Harper shifted Maya onto one arm and took a quick peek inside the bags. "No worries," she reassured him. "I see bread, eggs, milk and sandwich fixings. Fruit. Perfect. Nobody will starve."

"Hungwy," whined Maya hopefully around her blue teething toy.

Harper stroked her soft hair. "We'll fix you a nice snack." She sent a quick smile Linc's way. "Turn the heat on. We're fine."

"Great." He was already turning away.

There was a booster seat at the table. She put Maya in it, peeled a banana and gave the little girl half. Next, Harper found crayons and a tablet in a kitchen drawer. She handed them to Jayden and asked him to draw some pictures.

He had questions. "Pictures of what, Harper? How many pictures? What colors do you like? Should they be *Christmas* pictures?"

She tipped Maya's chin up. "What do you think your brother should draw for us?"

Maya swallowed a bite of banana and exclaimed, "Cwissmuss!"

Harper winked at Jayden. "You heard your sister. We want some Christmas pictures—in Christmas colors, like green and red and yellow." But why limit a guy's creativity? "Blue and purple and pink are perfectly acceptable, as well. In fact, Jayden, you should use any color in the box. I kind of love them all."

"A Christmas tree, Harper? A snowman?"

"Yes. Good ideas. Start with those." She pressed a kiss to Maya's silky hair just so she could breathe in the scent of baby shampoo and that special something else exclusive to little ones—like fresh, sweet milk and clean sheets hung to dry in the sunlight.

"More?" pleaded Maya, who had scarfed down the half banana in record time. Harper gave her the other half, found a plastic plate and a sippy cup in one of the cupboards and then supplemented the banana with dry cereal, sliced apples and milk.

Linc got the utilities turned on and the fire going in the gas fireplace. It wasn't long before the cottage warmed up enough that they could hang up their coats.

Harper kept both kids occupied as Linc got the rest of the stuff from the car and then started making beds.

As soon as Maya finished her snack, Harper

gave her back her chew toy and set her down on the kitchen floor, where she toddled around a bit and ended up plopping to her butt by the table. For a while, she just sat there cuddling the stuffed pig Linc had brought in from the car, contentedly chewing on the blue toy.

By then, Jayden had drawn a Christmas tree, a snowman and a picture of five smiling stick figures. "That's me and Maya and Uncle Linc and Gramma Jean and PopPop," the boy explained. "Gramma and PopPop just went on a boat to go everywhere around the whole world. They won't be back for a looong time."

Harper studied the smiling figures. "Are you saying your grandparents went on a cruise?"

"Yeah. A cruise. That's what they call it. They took care of us for a looong time and now they get to go on vacation, and we will be with Uncle Linc, but get to see them all the time on Stype."

"You mean Skype?"

Jayden wrinkled his nose, thinking it over. Finally, he nodded. "I think so, yes. Skype." He bent over the paper again and began to add what looked like a boat to the picture. "All done!" he announced.

Harper praised his work and then found some magnets in the drawer where the crayons had been. She hung all three pictures on the big two-door fridge. "They look great," she said. "Very festive."

Jayden frowned. "What's festive?"

"Happy and cheerful and jolly."

"Like you feel at Christmas?"

She nodded approvingly. "That's right."

Jayden beamed with pride. "Yes, my pictures are festive. And I like them, too."

"It's always nice to be pleased with your work. And now that the pictures are finished, I think we need to get started on dinner."

Jayden wanted to help, so Harper found him a step stool. He stood at the counter beside her, chattering away, munching on chips and nibbling on slices of cheese.

"I hewp, too!" insisted Maya midway through the process. She seemed pretty steady on her feet, so Harper let her stand on the other step stool, with Jayden on one side of her and Harper on the other. "I good!" announced the toddler as she chewed on a piece of bread.

"Yes, you are. Very helpful," Harper agreed.

When they all four sat down at the table, Linc praised the meal and the kids' efforts and confessed that he was having some serious trouble figuring out how to get the Wi-Fi working. "I may have to call the property manager," he added.

"I'm pretty good with anything technical," Harper volunteered. "Let me have a look at it first."

"Not only a kid whisperer, but you've got the tech handled, as well?"

"I guess you could say that, yeah." She explained her work at the Valentine Bay Theatre downtown. "I'm the theater's tech director, which means if it doesn't have to do with acting, I'm the one to talk to. We do several shows a year. With each one, we try to get the participation of every child in town."

Jayden seized the moment. "Uncle Linc, can I please be in the Christmas show? I was in the show last year and it was so much fun."

Linc turned to Harper. "So, the Christmas show would be at the Valentine Bay Theatre?"

"That's right." She gave Jayden a smile and suggested, "How about this? I'll discuss the Christmas show with your uncle later and then he'll talk it over with you."

Jayden glanced from Harper to Linc and back to Harper again. She could see the wheels turning in his head as he considered going all out to get an immediate yes.

But in the end, he gave it up. "You just let me know, Uncle Linc."

"Will do."

And then he couldn't resist one more push at the goal. "Because I really, really want to be in that show."

"I can see that." Linc was trying not to grin. "Now finish your sandwich."

After the meal, they all four cleared the table. Even Maya waddled back and forth carrying her sippy cup and *Little Mermaid* plastic plate to the sink.

"Bath time," Linc said.

Jayden objected. "We just had baths yesterday."

"Might as well freshen up after that long car ride."

Jayden moved on to bargaining. "Can I get bubbles?"

"Of course."

"Well, then, okay!"

Linc herded the kids upstairs. Harper stayed behind to wipe the counters and sweep bits of chips and apple from the floor.

With the kitchen tidy, she sorted out the Wi-Fi situation. It didn't take long to get the home network up and running.

After that, she couldn't think of anything else that needed doing immediately, though she was tempted to delay leaving any way she could. Her cottage always seemed too quiet, and it was so warm and cozy here. The kids were the cutest. And Linc was…

Well, never mind about Linc. She didn't need to go getting too excited about the temporary guy next door.

And come to think of it, maybe the kids' clothes needed stashing in drawers upstairs…

She caught herself—because putting things in drawers without being asked to do it verged on intrusive.

She'd been a good neighbor, done her bit to help Linc and the kids get settled in. Time to say goodnight.

At the top of the stairs, she followed the sounds of splashing and laughter to the hall bathroom.

"Harper!" Jayden called when she stopped in the

open bathroom doorway. He was in his pajamas and playing with Maya, who sat in the tub.

"Hawp!" Maya echoed.

They waved at her and Maya splashed with abandon, sending bathwater and bubbles flying everywhere. At this rate, Jayden would need dry pj's before heading to bed.

Linc, kneeling by the tub, turned to grin at Harper. His button-up was wet and he had a patch of bubbles dripping down his cheek. She laughed.

"What?" he demanded.

She touched her own cheek. "You've got bubbles…"

"No kidding." He wiped them away.

And then they both just stared at each other—for a while. Several seconds, at least. The sounds of the two kids laughing and Maya's splashing faded into the background.

It was just Harper and this amazingly great guy—a guy who looked like someone off the cover of *GQ* and treated his little niece and nephew like the most important people in the world.

Because they were.

"Wi-Fi's working," she said, her voice strangely breathless.

"Best news I've had since you organized dinner. We have a video-chat with the grandparents first thing in the morning. They're staying overnight in Miami, boarding a cruise ship tomorrow afternoon."

"Jayden mentioned a cruise."

"A cruise around the world, six months and thirty-three countries."

"Wow."

"Jean and Alan Hollister are the best there is. They canceled a two-week Mediterranean cruise last January to stay with me and the kids. The world cruise is my attempt to make it up to them."

Jean and Alan Hollister, he'd said. Gramma and PopPop must be Kevin's parents, not Linc and Megan's. "I'm sure they're going to love it—and the Wi-Fi is ready for your video call tomorrow. I left the password on a sticky note next to your laptop, but it's actually printed right there on the bottom of the gateway, too."

He gave a low chuckle. "See, I knew that…"

She tried not to giggle and found it a challenge to restrain herself. Something about him had her feeling like a thirteen-year-old in the throes of her first major crush. "Looks to me like you've got everything under control now."

"I hope so." He'd barely finished the sentence when Maya gave a gleeful screech and let loose a volley of wild splashing. Jayden splashed her back. "Whoa!" Linc swiped bubbles off his forehead. "How 'bout we keep the bubbles in the bathtub, guys?"

"Sow-wy," said Maya, looking completely angelic, with her curly hair sopping wet and topped with bubbles.

Linc's amber gaze fell on Harper again. "I have

no clue where you got the idea that I'm running this show."

"Hey. The kids are happy, and the beds are made. The Wi-Fi is working. Everybody's been fed. You're on top of this situation, and my job here is done."

The corners of his sexy mouth turned down just a fraction. "Wait. You're not leaving? You can't go yet."

"Yeah, Harper!" Jayden backed him up. "We still have stories. You have to stay for story time."

"Stow-ie!" shouted Maya, and then tossed her rubber frog in the air. It plopped back into the water with a splash. "Oopsy." She tried to look contrite but didn't really succeed.

Linc gave his niece an indulgent glance and swung those melty eyes back on Harper. "Are you vulnerable to a bribe?"

Absolutely. "Hmm. What's on offer?"

"Later, there will be wine—or vodka, if that's your preference."

"You have wine?" There hadn't been any in the grocery bags he'd brought in.

"I do. I just haven't brought it in from the car yet. The way I see it, so what if we only had sandwiches for dinner? At least I didn't forget the liquor."

It happened again. They stared at each other. It felt like…infinite possibility, somehow. Like she was floating on air, walking on rainbows. Like all the corny, lovely things a woman feels when she meets a certain special man.

And she really needed *not* to get carried away here. Linc was a great guy. They had a neighborly thing going on, not a budding romantic relationship.

But reading stories with the kids? That sounded like a lot more fun than returning to her empty cottage and going over the list of props she still hadn't found for the Christmas show. "Hmm. Wine. It just seems wrong to say no to wine…"

Those gorgeous eyes gleamed at her. "I think you've earned it."

"True. I've been such a good neighbor."

"The best." The kids laughed and chattered together as Linc and Harper continued to gaze at each other. His voice low, with a delicious hint of roughness, he coaxed, "Stay…"

Chapter Two

They had story time in the master bedroom, all four of them together on the king-size bed.

After *The Name Jar*, *Dragons Love Tacos* and an older book of rhymes by Shel Silverstein, both kids were droopy-eyed and yawning. Jayden asked Harper to tuck him in and Maya held up her arms for Linc, who scooped her against his broad chest and carried her to the bedroom across the hall.

Jayden took Harper's hand. "This way."

In his room, Harper pulled back the covers on the bottom bunk. He wiggled between them and stretched out with his head on the pillow. She tucked the Star Wars comforter in around him.

"Harper?"

"Hmm?"

"Sometimes in the nighttime, I miss my mom."

She smoothed the thick, dark hair from his forehead and whispered, "I really did like your mom a lot."

"She died. My daddy died, too." His eyes were wide and soft and full of hurt. "It makes me feel sad."

She laid her palm gently on the center of his small chest. "I remember that they both—your mom and your dad—loved you so much."

"I 'member that, too." His little face was so very solemn.

"That's good. Because when somebody loves you a lot, you never lose them. Not really. You always have them, the good memories of them, in your heart."

"Harper, I 'member *everything*."

"Keep those memories. Treasure them."

"I promise I will."

"Excellent. Do you have a prayer you like to say at bedtime?"

He closed his eyes and whispered, "Dear God, thank You for another good day. Please give us a tall Christmas tree and make the snow come down so I can have a snowman. Bless Uncle Linc and Maya and Gramma and PopPop. And Mom and Daddy up in heaven…" His dark lashes fluttered as he sneaked a peek at her. "And Harper, too. Amen."

"Amen." She bent to brush her lips across his forehead. "'Night."

"G'night—and Harper?"

"Yes?"

"Don't forget the Christmas show…"

"I won't forget. I'll talk to your uncle tonight."

When Harper got downstairs, she found Linc in the kitchen pulling bottles from a box.

He held up a bottle of red and another of Ketel One. "Pick your poison."

"Wine, please."

He put the vodka back in the box. "Let's go in by the fire," he suggested, after he'd opened the wine and she'd found two stemless glasses in one of the cupboards.

In the living area, they sat on the sofa and he poured them each a glass. "It's good," she said after her first sip.

They sat in silence for a bit. She hardly knew him, and yet it was easy to sit with him and say nothing, to simply enjoy the warmth of the fire and the rich, dark taste of the wine.

Her thoughts went to the little boy upstairs and the things he'd said before his bedtime prayer. "While I was tucking him in, Jayden said how much he missed his mom and dad…" She waited for a response.

None was forthcoming. Linc stared at the fire and took another slow sip of wine.

Okay. Now she did feel awkward. "The kids seem to be doing really well."

He slanted her a wry glance. "Given that they lost both their parents ten and a half months ago, you mean?"

"Yeah." She wanted to reach out, touch his hand, pat his big shoulder. But that seemed presumptuous, somehow. Instead, she struggled with how to offer her condolences. "I'm so sorry, Linc. That you lost them. I met them last year, over Christmas."

"Yeah. I figured you must have gotten to know them a little. Jayden mentioned hanging out with you and your sister last year."

"I thought they were wonderful, both Megan and Kevin. So in love. Good parents, completely committed to their family, to the kids…"

"Yeah. It's been hard, losing them. Jayden acted up some at first. There were angry outbursts, essentially out of nowhere, and sudden bouts of crying. I talked it over with Jean and Alan. We decided to send him to a therapist. That helped."

"Right now, he really does seem happy, overall."

"Yeah, he's coping, I think." Linc had resumed staring into the fire. "I didn't get together with my sister and her family enough before the crash. I regret that now, that I didn't make the time to fly down to Sacramento now and then…"

Anything she might have said felt either inadequate or shallow, so she said nothing.

He didn't seem bothered by her silence. "I don't

know how I would have made it these past months without Jean and Alan," he said. "They left their cozy place in Carmichael, California, and moved in with me in the West Hills to help me look after the kids."

There were a lot of big houses in the West Hills of Portland. Harper had no doubt that Linc's was one of them.

He said, "Having their grandparents taking care of them gave Jayden and Maya time to adjust to the new normal, I guess you could say." He shifted his gaze down and seemed to contemplate the dark color of the wine. Shaking his head, he took another sip. Then a grim laugh escaped him. "Kevin loved that damn plane of his. It was his pride and joy…"

"I heard about what happened." The Hollisters had left the kids with the grandparents in Sacramento and flown off for an overnight getaway in Monterey. They'd crashed in the Santa Cruz Mountains and were killed instantly.

"It was a shock," he said. "To everyone. I don't really think we're over it yet."

Again, she had to resist the urge to reach out—clasp his arm, pat his shoulder. "Something like that, you never really get over. But it does get better—you know, over time."

He turned his gaze on her, his eyes darker than before, more bittersweet chocolate than caramel. "You sound like you're speaking from experience."

"Yeah, you could say that…"

The way he looked at her—as though she fascinated him. How did he do that? He made her feel
seen in the truest sense of the word. "Tell me," he
commanded.

She shifted on the cushions and took another sip
of her wine. "When I was five, my brother Finn got
lost in Siberia. Then, when I was seven, my parents
died." She chuckled at the look of disbelief on his
face. "My parents were big on travel. Finn was eight
when he disappeared. We're still looking to this day,
but we haven't found him. Yet. Two years after we
lost Finn, my parents headed off on a romantic getaway, just the two of them, to Thailand. As my oldest brother, Daniel, always explained it to the rest of
us, the Thailand trip was supposed to be a way for
them to reconnect with each other, to try to move on
a little after Finn went missing. They arrived right
in time to be killed in a tsunami."

"That's horrible."

"It was, yeah. But we got through it. There were
eight of us at home then, including Daniel. Daniel
took custody of the rest of us. Our ancient great-
aunt, Daffy, and great-uncle, Percy, were always
there to help. Daffy and Percy are the Bravo family's
Gramma Jean and PopPop, I guess you could say."

He was still watching her, his expression hard to
read. "Thank you."

"For...?"

He gave a half shrug. "Sometimes I forget I'm
not the only one who ever lost a sibling. I get feeling

down, remembering all the ways I wasn't there for Megan when I should have been, worrying the kids will never fully recover from losing her and their dad. But you've made it through more than one personal tragedy as a child and grown up with a great attitude. Not to mention, you're generous and kind, and willing to come to the rescue of the clueless guy next door. So, yeah. Thank you for all of that." He tapped his glass to hers.

"I never said I thought you were clueless."

His mouth quirked at the corners. "But you did think it, didn't you?"

"Maybe. At first. But you're good with the kids, and it's clear they love you and trust you."

His grin had turned rueful. "I have a confession to make."

She held up her wineglass in a salute. "Now you're talkin'. Spill."

"Jean tried to tell me I would need help for the holidays, but I wouldn't listen to her. I was positive I could do it all, get the cottage opened up, run to the grocery store, look after Jayden and Maya—and fit in working remotely a few hours a day, too. Today was a crash course in harsh reality."

"You might have been maybe a touch too ambitious."

"You think?" He laughed, a low sound, intimate. Just between the two of them.

She tried to remind herself—again—that she'd only just met him. He was a Stryker, an important name in Oregon, and only here for the holidays. Come New Year's, he'd be gone. Back to Portland to live in a West Hills mansion and run his family's shipping empire. She would be heading for Seattle, where she would rent an overpriced studio apartment and try to figure out what she really wanted from life.

Didn't matter, though, how mindful she tried to be of all the ways they were strangers. Somehow, in the span of an afternoon and evening, she felt as though she'd known him for years.

He smiled his devastating smile. "Jayden chattered nonstop all the way here from Portland."

"Why am I not surprised? He's wonderfully verbal."

"Verbal." Linc shrugged. "That's Jayden, all right. And my point is, all the way here, you and your sister were the main topic of his never-ending monologue. He couldn't wait to see you. He has all these plans for hanging out with you—for building snowmen and being in your Christmas show…"

"Which reminds me, I promised him I'd talk to you about the show."

"Don't worry. If you think it's a good thing, I'll say yes. I'm pretty much incapable of telling Jayden no."

"Well, I'm not arguing that you can *never* say no. But the Christmas show should be a definite yes. He starts kindergarten next year, right?" At his nod, she continued, "So next Christmas, you won't be able to stay the whole month. He shouldn't miss this chance. He'll get to be around a lot of other kids and the rehearsal schedule isn't all that demanding. You could start him next week if you want to wait until after Thanksgiving."

"Hold on. The rehearsals have already started? How will he catch up?"

"It's a series of sketches, songs and dance numbers. My sister Hailey directs the whole thing. She's amazing—and I say that with absolute objectivity."

"Right."

"I'm serious. She has the kids practice all the songs and skits separately, in small groups, and then puts everything together during the last week before the show opens. We will fit Jayden in, and he'll have a wonderful time. He'll need to be at the theater for a few hours most weekday afternoons, depending on which numbers he's in. There are two performances, both matinees, on the second and third Saturdays of December. I can hook you up for carpooling with other parents. Once you're comfortable with the process, you don't need to be there if you don't want to be. Jayden will be busy with his part in the show and there's constant adult supervision. Even Maya's old enough to participate this year."

He frowned. "She's barely two."

"I know. But if they can walk and understand basic instructions, they're in. The older kids love looking after the little ones, kind of shepherding them along. Maya can be in a couple of sketches if she's comfortable with it. That would take a little more time on your part—or for anyone you get to look after the kids. Children four and under require a supervising adult for each rehearsal they attend."

"What about the performances? She could wet her diaper, start crying…"

"Linc, it ain't Broadway. Everybody understands. You would just go up onstage and get her, take her out to the lobby to settle her down or whatever. Meanwhile, the show would go on." She set her glass on the coffee table.

He put his down beside it and poured them each more wine. "I'll tell Jayden he's in." At some point, he'd rolled his sleeves to his elbows. His forearms were the good kind—corded with lean muscle, traced with a couple of so-sexy veins and dusted with just the right amount of silky dark hair. He had gorgeous wrists, too, lean, the bones sharply defined.

And seriously? Gorgeous *wrists*? She should probably say no to that second glass of wine…

And what were they talking about…?

Right. He'd just said that Jayden could be in the show. "Terrific. He'll be so pleased."

"I'll have to think a little about putting Maya in."

"I hear you. I'll give you my number." She took out her phone, entered her PIN and handed it to him.

He sent himself a text. On the coffee table, his phone chimed. "Done." He passed her phone back and relaxed against the cushions again, wineglass in hand. "I need to ask you…"

Anything. "Yeah?"

"Last year, did you maybe babysit the kids now and then?"

"Yes, I did. It was fun—and you should see your face."

"What's wrong with it?" His slight grin let her know he was teasing her.

"Nothing wrong, exactly. But I do detect a calculating gleam in your eye."

"You're onto me." He studied her for a long count of five. "Jayden and Maya adore you. You're amazing with kids."

"Um. Thanks?"

"And I'm facing reality here, admitting that I do need a nanny while we're in town. Will you consider taking the job? Flexible hours, whatever you can manage. As I already said, you're so good with them, and you're also right next door. You could just come on over anytime you're available."

She sipped that second glass of wine she shouldn't be having and considered the idea. She did enjoy being with the kids…

He coaxed, "Say yes. I'll definitely make it worth your while in terms of the money."

Now he'd done it—found her weak spot. She needed to save every penny she could get her hands on for her upcoming move. "You have an hourly rate in mind?"

"Eighty an hour?"

She tried not to gape. His offer was a lot more

than she'd dared to hope for. "I could come in the afternoons. Mornings, I need to be at the theater. And then some days I would switch, watch the kids in the morning, go to the theater in the afternoon."

"As I said, whenever you're available, I'm grateful for the help."

He'd pretty much had her at that giant hourly rate. Still, he needed to understand that she did require flexibility in terms of her schedule. "I really can't work for you full-time."

"You already said that, and I heard you."

"You're sure?"

"Positive. Jayden and Maya love you, and you're so good with them. If you could be here every weekday for a few hours—and longer whenever you can manage it? That would give me the time I need to put out any fires at Stryker Marine."

She suddenly felt hesitant, somehow.

But why? She needed the money and he could use the help. Plus, it would be no hardship for her to spend time with Maya and Jayden.

She would have to sock away every penny she could get her hands on to achieve her goal and make her move by February, and this was a golden opportunity to fatten her malnourished bank account.

Linc leaned a fraction closer. She got a hint of his aftershave. Fresh and clean and manly. He was way too attractive. And too rich. She'd read somewhere that he'd been CEO and President of Stryker Marine Transport since he was twenty-five. "Harper."

"Hmm?"

"Just say yes."

Oh, come on. Why not? Instead of spending hours alone at her cottage, she could be here making excellent money, taking care of two great kids for this way-too-attractive man. "Yes."

His smile made her pulse speed up. "Can you start tomorrow afternoon?"

"Yes."

"Excellent. You just made my month—oh, and I have meetings I can't get out of in Portland on Thursday and Friday the first week in December. Any chance you could spend the two days there with me and the kids at my house, looking after them while I'm at the office? I would pay you for eighteen hours a day on those two days if you can swing it."

She did the math. Almost three thousand dollars for two days. She would have to work it out with Hailey and Doug Dickerson. The theater's volunteer lighting director, Doug would be stepping up into Harper's job when she left in February. "Sure. I'll make it work."

"You're a lifesaver. Don't move from that spot. I'll get you a key and grab my laptop. We'll download a simple contract, fill in the blanks to our mutual satisfaction and be good to go."

After Harper left, Linc checked on the kids. They were both sound asleep, looking so pure and innocent, untroubled by the hard realities of life. He went into the master suite and spent about thirty seconds staring at the king-size bed. The duvet was rumpled from the four of them—Harper, the kids and him—lying there together to read bedtime stories.

Linc glanced at his watch. It was barely nine.

He could get a head start on messages before he turned in, find out more than he wanted to know about how everyone at the office was getting along in his absence.

Downstairs again, he got his laptop from the office room and returned to the living area, where he sat on the sofa and started checking email and messages. Harper would be over around one tomorrow. She'd said she could stay into the evening if he needed her.

He would absolutely need her.

Maybe after the kids went to bed, they could hang out for a while, the way they had tonight. He really liked her. She was not only a pleasure to look at, she was easygoing, capable and fun. And smart. With a big heart. Low maintenance, too, in her floppy sweater, ripped skinny jeans and high-top Converse All Stars.

He'd been swimming in the wrong dating pool. There should be more women like Harper Bravo in his life.

On the coffee table next to his laptop, his phone chimed with a text. He tapped the text icon.

Imogen's profile shot popped up, a picture he'd taken at a charity gala they'd attended together last year, before Megan died and everything changed. Imogen wore a strapless red satin dress. A diamond necklace he'd given her sparkled at her throat and the big rock in her engagement ring glittered on her left hand as she coyly blew him a kiss.

Imogen was a lot like Linc's mother, Alicia—completely self-absorbed. He should have taken note of that before getting involved with her.

But he hadn't. And less than a week ago, he'd finally had to face the fact that Imogen Whitman was not the woman for him. She was the one who broke it off, but he'd been way too relieved when she did. They weren't a good match. He got that now.

He shouldn't read her text. There was no point. But he couldn't help wondering what she might pull next.

I was upset. I'm sorry for the things I said. We really need to talk.

Bad idea. They never needed to talk again. Everything had been settled. *She* needed to let it go.

He went back to dealing with his messages.

A second text popped through.

Linc. Come on. The least you can do is answer me.

He blocked her from his mind—and if she kept it up, he would block her number from his phone.

The phone rang. He should just let it go to voice

mail and then delete whatever message she left. But he was pissed off and he wanted to make himself utterly clear.

He hit the green icon and put the phone to his ear. "It's over. Stop texting me. Don't call me again."

"Oh, Linc." Her voice was soft. Pleading—which was rich. There was nothing soft about Imogen Whitman. He understood that now. "Come on. We can work this—"

He didn't hang on for the rest. Ending the call, he blocked her.

The next morning, Harper arrived at the landmark theater on Carmel Street good and early. Hailey was already there.

Harper's sister sat in her office backstage sipping a latte from their favorite coffee place, the Steamy Bean, and studying an Excel spreadsheet on her tablet. "Roman wants to close us down as soon as the Christmas show's over to start the remodel," she said without looking up. "I told him that now the theater is mine to do with as I please, I have things in the works. He'll need to renovate around upcoming projects. He says that's impossible, that the wiring alone means just about every wall has to be ripped out."

Roman Marek was Hailey's fiancé. A real estate guy, Roman was prone to larger-than-life gestures. A few weeks ago, he'd given Hailey the theater. Now he was determined to refurbish it to her specifications. They were at odds over how that would happen.

"You'll work it out, Lee-Lee." Harper used the old nickname, from when they were little—Harp and Lee-Lee, like twins, inseparable. "You always do."

Hailey sat up straight, the spreadsheet forgotten, and narrowed her eyes at Harper. "Okay. What's on your mind?" Hailey was ten months older, but they might as well have been born ten minutes apart.

They'd been a team all through childhood. Their mom had even held Hailey back a year so she and Harper could start kindergarten together. They went off to the University of Oregon together, both as theater majors—Hailey focusing on performance, directing and management, Harper on stagecraft and design—and her other great love, architecture. They finished each other's sentences. And sometimes they read each other's minds.

Harper dropped into the straight chair opposite Hailey's vintage metal desk. "I took a second job and I wanted to let you know. It's flexible, a few hours a day, after I'm done here at the theater."

"You're never done here at the theater."

"Yeah, well. I'll make it work. You know I need the money. A place in Seattle won't be cheap." She watched Hailey closely as she spoke, on the lookout for any hint that her sister wasn't really down with the move she had planned. It would, after all, break them up in terms of their partnership as H&H Productions. And for the first time in their lives, they would be living miles apart.

But Lee-Lee didn't so much as flinch. Harper

loved her all the more for that. Her sister knew what Harper needed, and she wanted Harper to have it. "I hear you. So then, you'll be making good money at this mysterious second job?"

"Eighty bucks an hour."

Hailey's right eyebrow inched toward her hairline. "Do you have to take your clothes off?"

"Oh, please. To do that, I would need more than eighty an hour." They laughed together and then Harper asked, "Remember the Hollister kids?"

"Of course." Hailey's teasing expression had turned somber. "It's heartbreaking, what happened to Megan and Kevin."

"Yeah." For a bittersweet moment, they regarded each other. Memories of the sweet couple from Sacramento seemed to hover in the air between them. Megan had had a glow about her. You could see that her life made her happy. And Kevin was kind of nerdy and a little bit shy. With a long breath, Harper forged on, "Megan's brother, Linc Stryker, took custody of Jayden and Maya. He's brought the kids to the Stryker cottage for the holidays. Last night, he offered me a job as part-time nanny while they're here in town."

"Wait." Hailey made a rolling gesture with her hand. "I need you to back it up a little. You met Megan's brother, how?" Harper gave her sister a quick rundown on the events of the day before, after which Hailey asked, "Is this brother of Megan's single?"

Harper realized she didn't know. He'd certainly

acted like he was single—hadn't he? "He's alone with the kids at the cottage. He didn't mention a girlfriend and he doesn't wear a ring, so I'm guessing, yes."

As always, Hailey saw right through her. "You like him. You like him a lot."

Had her face turned red? She willed the blush away. "I hardly know the man—I mean, he seems nice."

"Nice." Hailey wrinkled her nose like she smelled something bad.

"Yeah. Nice. And I do like him."

Hailey smirked. "He's hot, am I right?"

"Will you stop?" She'd been thinking way too much about the guy next door and she needed to cut that out. Especially now that she would be working for him. Romance in the workplace was not a great idea. She could lose a fun gig taking care of two kids she really liked—not to mention the money she now counted on putting in the bank.

"So, then." Hailey sat back in her swivel chair. "He's hot and you like him and you're going to be hanging around him a lot in the next month—for purely financial reasons."

"Enough. I've got a lot of work to do and a short time to do it in." Harper rose and turned for the door.

"Say hi to Jayden for me and be sure to give Maya a great, big kiss…"

Harper sent a wave back over her shoulder and kept right on walking.

* * *

The doorbell rang at one sharp.

Linc answered and there she was, in baggy, busted-out jeans and a black waffle-weave shirt. She carried a puffer coat the color of marigolds and she'd woven her thick, streaky blond hair into a single fat braid that fell over her left shoulder, the tail teasing the undercurve of one round breast. He wanted to grab that braid and give it a tug.

He stepped back and ushered her in. "Here. I'll take your coat."

"Thanks." She handed it over. A hint of her scent came to him—sweet and tart, like vanilla and lemons.

As he hung the coat in the entry closet, Jayden came running. "Harper, *there* you are!"

Maya trailed after him, crowing, "Hawp, Hawp!"

Harper laughed—she seemed delighted at the sight of the two kids barreling toward her. "Hey, you guys!"

She knelt to gather them both in a quick hug. They wiggled like excited puppies in her loose embrace. When she stood, she scooped Maya up on one arm and took Jayden's offered hand.

"We don't get the Christmas tree until Friday because first there's Thanksgiving," Jayden said.

"That makes sense."

"And I get to be in the Christmas show," he proudly informed her. "Uncle Linc said so."

"I'm glad."

"Me, too. And we had a Skype with PopPop and

Gramma Jean before they got on the big boat to go out in the ocean—now, come up to my room." He started pulling her toward the stairs. "I built a whole train station. Uncle Linc helped. The train tracks click together, and you can make them go everywhere, even under my bed."

"I want to see that—but hold on a minute."

"What for?"

"I need to talk to your uncle first." She planted a quick kiss on Maya's cheek. Then she turned those big eyes on Linc. "Have they had lunch?"

"We did!" Jayden tugged on her hand again, this time to get her attention. "We had eggs and toast for breakfast, and we had sandwiches for lunch, with chips. Now we're all out of chips, though," he added with a frown. "And there's no more ham. We'll have to have chicken sandwiches for dinner, I guess. I don't like chicken, not as much as ham."

Linc felt a twinge of guilt. He should have gone shopping this morning, but he kind of dreaded dragging the kids around Safeway while trying to find everything they might need for several days of meals. In Portland, he had a cook who took care of that stuff.

But this was the cottage, he reminded himself. It was family-only around here—well, except that he'd hired Harper, which made the family-only rule pretty much null and void.

Not that he regretted hiring her. No way. She was a find and would make it possible for him to get a little work done now and then while giving the kids the kind of Christmas they deserved.

As for the shopping, it had to be done, which meant that this afternoon, along with resolving the never-ending issues at the office, he would need to haul his ass to the store.

He was about to reassure Harper he would deal with the food situation when she volunteered, "Trust me to take care of it?" A matched pair of sweet little dimples winked at him from either side of her beautiful mouth.

The woman *was* a prize. As generous and helpful as Gramma Jean, and gorgeous, as well. "You're not serious?"

"The kids and I would love a trip to the store— wouldn't we, guys?"

"Yes!" the two little ones said in unison.

Harper suggested, "Just jot down a grocery list for me, if you would."

"You're a lifesaver."

She shrugged. "No problem. Does Maya need a nap?"

Did she? He had no clue. "Jean wrote it all down for me, in longhand on the pretty stationery she uses—about naps and allergies and when to do what. I'm fairly sure I brought those instructions with me from Portland…"

Harper seemed amused at his befuddlement. "Well, okay then. If you find it, let me know. Otherwise, I think we'll go for groceries soon and then we'll figure out the nap issue when we get back."

"Works for me. I'll put the shopping list together right now. Just add anything else you want or think I should have included."

"Like chips!" Jayden put in. "We could get Fritos. I *like* Fritos."

"Fweetos!" Maya echoed, clearly in agreement with her big brother.

Linc whipped out his black card and grabbed his keys from the art glass bowl on the entry table. "The kids' car seats are already hooked up in the Range Rover. You might as well just drive that."

"Works for me." Harper let go of Jayden's hand to take the card and keys. Her fingers brushed Linc's, light as a breath, sending an arrow of awareness slicing through him.

Was he way too attracted to her?

Probably.

Not that there was anything wrong with that. He and Imogen were yesterday's news, so what harm could there be in a little innocent flirting with the new nanny? It put a whole new light on the day, just having her around. He had no plans to make a move on her. None whatsoever.

As soon as she'd stuck the keys and credit card in her pocket, Jayden grabbed her hand again. "Harper. Can I please show you my train set now?"

She grinned down at his upturned face. "Lead the way, young man." He pulled her toward the stairs.

Linc remembered he had more to discuss with her. "Hold on a minute…"

She sent him a glowing smile over her shoulder. "Hmm?"

"About Maya and the Christmas show…"

"You think you might let her try it?"

"Well, I wondered if you could take her, be there for whatever practices she needs to attend—on the clock, of course? I thought you would see how she does with it, make a judgment call from there."

"I, me, Maya?" Maya had evidently understood enough of his words to get that they were discussing her.

Harper nuzzled her cheek. "Yes, you, Maya. It's going to be such fun."

"I fun!"

"You certainly are," Harper agreed. She turned that blinding, happy smile on Linc again. "That's a great idea. I'll talk to Hailey tonight, see where she can fit them both in. I might even be able to take them to their first rehearsal tomorrow afternoon."

"That works."

The eager Jayden was pulling on her hand again. "Come on, Harper…"

She laughed as the little boy led her away.

Harper's plan was to work as many hours as possible for Linc. If she put in only twenty hours a week, she could add seven thousand dollars toward her moving fund by New Year's—more, when she included the two eighteen-hour days he would pay her for when she watched the kids in Portland.

That day, she did the shopping, cooked the dinner and hung around for face-washing, toothbrushing, story time and tucking the kids in. Seven hours total. More days like today and her moving fund would cease to be a problem.

Linc waited at the foot of the stairs when she came down. He looked distractingly hunky in his dark-wash jeans and gray-blue sweater, the sleeves pushed to his elbows—and uh-uh. She was not letting herself get carried away admiring his forearms and mentally rhapsodizing over his manly wrists.

"So, then," she said, all business. "Tomorrow, I'll be here at—"

"Stay," he interrupted, his warm gaze holding hers. "Just for a little while."

She really had planned to keep it strictly professional, but for some reason, her mouth opened of its own accord and the wrong word popped out. "Sure."

Hey. No big deal. He probably needed to talk about something concerning the kids.

Linc offered wine. She accepted. Nothing wrong with that. She deserved a little treat at the end of the day. She and Hailey used to go out for beers after work three or four times a week, back before Hailey met Roman.

Really, Harper spent too many evenings alone nowadays. Why shouldn't she enjoy a late happy hour with her new boss?

In the living room by the fire, he poured her a glass of wine and then some for himself. They settled back against the cushions.

For several minutes, they sipped in silence. Like the night before, it was nice, easy. Comfortable.

When she glanced at him, she saw he was hiding a grin and his eyes had a teasing light in them. She liked that light, maybe too much.

"There's a turkey in my fridge," he said.

She turned her body his way and hitched a knee up onto the cushions. "It wasn't on the list, but I kind of figured you would need a bird for Thursday. I also got cranberries for sauce and stuff for dressing. Plus sweet potatoes and string beans—all the sides you could possibly hope for."

He frowned. "Wait a minute. You're talking about Thanksgiving dinner?"

"Sorry. I assumed you would be cooking, and you said to add anything I thought you might need."

He seemed vaguely embarrassed. "Can I be brutally honest?"

Brutally? That didn't sound very encouraging. "Of course."

"I was just going to get takeout. Is that sad or what?" His brow crinkled even more. "There's gotta be a place in town that's open on Thursday. Right?"

"Yeah. But you should order by tomorrow. I'll text you some suggestions."

"You're a lifesaver."

She laughed. "Don't overpraise me. I'll become impossible to work with."

"I doubt it. You sure you don't want to move to Portland and look after the kids for me full-time?"

Why was that idea so tempting? And why was she leaning into him—close enough to smell his wonderful scent, woodsy with a hint of spice, and make out the gold flecks in his brown eyes? Reluctantly, she lowered her foot to the floor and turned her body toward the fire again. "I love taking care of Maya and Jayden. But I don't really think I'm career nanny material."

He faked a big sigh. "Go ahead. Crush all my hopes—and you know what? I'm fairly sure there's a cookbook or two around here. I'm going to grow a pair and figure out how to roast that turkey myself."

She didn't know which sounded sadder—Linc and the kids having takeout, just the three of them, on the holiday where families gathered close around a big, home-cooked meal. Or him cooking Thanksgiving dinner for the first time by himself.

Don't do it, Harp, she berated herself. *Don't you dare do it.*

But the image of him and Maya and Jayden alone with a burned turkey and some singed sweet potatoes on Thanksgiving Day made it impossible for her to keep her mouth shut. "Look. We have a huge family dinner up at my brother Daniel's house on Thanksgiving. It's the more the merrier. There will be lots of kids, plenty of great food and nice wine. Why don't you join us?"

He didn't say a word for several seconds. She just knew he was going to say no to her invitation. She should be relieved about that, but instead she braced herself to feel let down.

"I have to confess," he said at last.

"Hey." She kept it light. "It was only a suggestion. We'd love to have you, but I understand if you want it to be just the three of you."

He gave a low chuckle, an intimate sound that made her feel all warm inside. "Are you kidding? We would love to come."

Her unacceptable disappointment vanished like morning mist in sunlight. "Great."

"As for my confession, I was trying really hard to make you take pity on me. I might feel a little guilty about manipulating you—but not guilty enough to let you off the hook now that you've offered to let me and the kids crash your family party."

She slanted him a chiding glance. "You were playing me."

"And I'm so glad that it worked. I pictured you at some big family dinner, and I couldn't help wishing I could give that kind of Thanksgiving to the kids."

She whacked his rock-hard shoulder with the back of her hand. "I can't believe you set me up."

He laughed again. "It's too late now. We're invited. You can't take it back." He picked up the wine bottle, offering her more. She held out her glass. As he poured, he asked, "So what do we do with the turkey and all the other stuff you bought?"

"No worries. It won't go to waste." She indulged in a slow, delicious sip. "I'll take some of it to Daniel's, if that's okay?"

"Of course."

"We all try to bring something, so I'll bring what I bought with your money." She gave him a flirty little smile with that.

"You're a crafty one." He said it admiringly.

"Oh, you better believe it." Really, she was having far too much fun—and she probably ought to slow down on the wine.

He'd rested his arm along the back of the sofa. She could feel the weight and warmth of it there, behind her shoulders, and she liked having him so close. All cozy and companionable.

Hailey was right. It was just possible that she might have a slight crush on her temporary boss.

This girl.

What *was* it about her?

It just felt so easy with her—and yet with an edge of excitement, too.

He probably shouldn't compare her to Imogen, but he did it anyway. Had he ever had fun with his ex-fiancée? He asked himself the question and kind of wished he hadn't. Imogen could be charming and friendly when it suited her purposes.

But she'd never been someone who just liked

hanging out. For the life of him, he couldn't imagine bringing her here to the cottage. She would have been bored out of her skull within an hour of walking in the door.

He wondered at himself sometimes—at how damn oblivious he could be. Oblivious enough that he hadn't even realized how unhappy he was with the woman he planned to marry. He'd been too busy working to realize that he was turning into his father and that Imogen had all the makings of Alicia Stryker 2.0—meaning even colder and even more calculating than his mother.

And then he'd lost his sister and become the guardian of the two sweetest kids on the planet, after which he'd spent ten months living in the same house with Jean and Alan and found out what a real marriage was.

The bald truth? When Imogen got fed up with him putting the kids first and dumped him, he'd dodged a bullet. Being around Harper brought that hard fact sharply home.

He sipped more wine and wondered about the pretty woman on the sofa beside him.

She slanted him a quick smile and then stared into the fire again. It was quiet in the big room. And it felt good, just to sit here beside her, saying nothing. Harper was someone who enjoyed the moment. She didn't waste any energy looking for somewhere better to be—the latest, hottest restaurant or a trip to fashion week in Manhattan.

Was she with someone? He couldn't stop himself from wondering.

She'd never mentioned a guy…

But why would she, necessarily? It might feel like he'd known her a long time, but they'd only just met.

He didn't like wondering if she might already belong to someone. Could it be that the sole reason she sat here next to him now was because he'd asked her to stay? He *was* her boss, after all. Until the end of the year, anyway.

No.

She didn't have anyone. She couldn't. He would know if she did…

Wouldn't he?

That he even dared to assume such a thing should have been ridiculous to him.

She turned to him again. Those beautiful baby blue eyes had him thinking of clear summer afternoons and the Pacific Ocean on a windless day.

And what was his problem here, really? A simple question would resolve this issue one way or another. "Got someone special waiting for you back at that cottage of yours?"

She looked at him so steadily. "I used to share it with my sister, but now I'm there on my own."

"No boyfriend trying to talk you into moving in with him?"

Her thick eyelashes swept down and then fluttered up. "No."

Warmth radiated through him. He'd been right.

There was no one. But he double-checked, just to be sure. "Not seeing anyone at the moment, then?"

Her mouth curved sweetly in a smile that seemed a little bit sad. "Not for a while. I was with a guy at UO. We broke up my senior year."

"Why?"

She stared into the fire again. "Let's just say that he and I grew apart."

It was an obvious evasion. He hoped she might get honest about it.

And then she did. "Okay, the truth is, he and I were never all that close. I was interested in my studies, in the next design problem I needed to solve— whether as a set builder or for a project in a 3D modeling class. It was nice to have someone to be with now and then, but he wasn't exactly the love of my life."

"You sound sad when you talk about him."

"Yeah, well. Most women my age have been in love at least once. For me, there have been dates and hookups and two steady boyfriends—the guy at UO and a boy I went out with in high school. But I've never actually found that special someone—you know, the man I would drop everything for. I've always had interesting work I wanted to do, my sister for a BFF and a big family to count on. Men have kind of taken a back seat in my life, you know?"

He got that. In a lot of ways, he was the same— minus the big family and the sister who was also a best friend. He had loved his sister, but once they grew up, they'd chosen different paths. Until Megan and Kevin went down in that plane, his life had centered on Stryker Marine.

"What about you?" she asked. "Anyone special?"

He'd figured that was coming. Still, he hesitated, though he knew it would be better just to put it right out there. Rip the bandage off, so to speak.

"Trying to decide how much to say?" she teased.

He went ahead and busted himself. "You got me."

Her big eyes had grown wary. "So there *is* someone, then?"

"No—but I was engaged until recently."

She blinked. Probably not a good sign. "How recently?"

"We broke up last Friday."

Chapter Three

Last Friday?

Until four days ago, Linc was engaged?

Harper couldn't hide her dismay. "What happened?"

He didn't answer immediately. She knew he was choosing his words with care and that did not reassure her. "I realized we weren't a good match, after all."

"So you just ended it?"

"No. *She* did—and that's good. As I said, we wouldn't have been happy together."

She wanted to know more, every detail. Who was this woman? How long were they together? Why had his fiancée broken it off just as he conveniently decided that the engagement wouldn't work?

And hold on a damn minute here…

Eighty bucks an hour, she reminded herself.

She needed to remember her goals. And her goals did not include getting too personal with Linc. Yeah, she liked him and she felt drawn to him.

But why take the chance she might ruin a good thing? This great job watching the kids could blow up in her face. She needed *not* to get too close.

The man was in flux. He'd been *engaged* until Friday.

Exactly, a devilish voice in the back of her mind cut in. *That could mean he not only needs a nanny to look after his adorable niece and nephew, Linc Stryker just might be a prime candidate for a rebound fling.*

They could have a good time. It could be just for fun, until New Year's, in the evenings, like now, when the kids were in bed.

And it could be good for her, too—like a Christmas present to herself. Something sweet and hot and temporary…

No.

Bad idea. It was just too risky.

Eighty bucks an hour.

She would make that her mantra every time she got carried away gazing into those warm brown eyes, longing to hear all his secrets, wanting to feel those perfect, hard arms wrapped around her and those sexy lips pressed to hers…

"Hey." He looked worried now. "You're very quiet…"

She set down her empty glass. When he moved to pour her some more, she put her hand over it. "I should go."

He tipped his head to the side, studying her. "The very recently broken engagement kind of freaked you out, huh?"

"No…"

"Don't lie." He said it so gently, and that caused an ache in the center of her chest.

Why? Nothing at all had been lost.

Yet she felt something really good slipping away.

Carefully, she guided her heavy braid back over her shoulder. "Well, I guess what you just told me did remind me that we have a great thing going here. You get help with the kids and I get to beef up my savings. Getting too close to each other could mess with the program, you know?"

"Not if we both went into it with our eyes wide-open."

A hot shiver raced down her spine. She sat back away from him. "What does that even mean?" she demanded, though she knew very well what it meant. A moment ago, she'd been thinking the same thing.

He said nothing for several seconds. When he did speak, it was cautiously. "I've offended you. I'm sorry. I really like you, Harper. Maybe too much. I find myself behaving in contradictory ways."

Her heart kind of melted. "Oh, Linc. I like *you*—and you surprised me, is all."

"Be specific." It was a command. His take-charge tone sent another giddy little shiver sliding down her spine.

She answered him honestly. "Well, a minute ago, I was thinking along the same lines as you, that maybe we could, you know, get together, just for fun, until New Year's."

Now he looked kind of mournful. "But then you realized that would be a bad idea?"

She nodded. "Too risky." They shared a long, intense look. The things they didn't say hung in the air between them. "I need this job with you, Linc." He gave her a slow nod in response. She rose. "And I'd better get going."

He walked her to the foyer, where he held her coat for her like the gentleman he was. "See you tomorrow."

"'Night, Linc." Pulling her coat closer around her, she went out into the chilly darkness.

Harper arrived on Linc's doorstep at one o'clock sharp the next day.

Her plan? To get the kids and get out.

In the evening, she would cook dinner if he needed her for that—and head straight back to her cottage as soon as the kids had been tucked in.

Absolutely no hanging around for wine by the fire.

But first, Linc had to be brought up to speed on her schedule for the day and on the Bravo family Thanksgiving tomorrow. She had the key he'd given her, but she rang the bell just to give him fair warning that she'd arrived. As she let herself in, he appeared in the arch to the living area, wearing a sweater the same honey-brown as his eyes and perfectly fitted dark-wash jeans that probably cost more than the costume budget for the Christmas show. Maya toddled along beside him.

"Hey." He gave her a cautious smile.

"Hey."

"Hawp!" Maya came right to her.

Harper scooped her up. "How you doin', pretty girl?"

"I pwetty!" She wrapped her little arms around Harper's neck.

"*So* pretty," Harper agreed. She asked Linc, "Where's Jayden?"

"In his room playing with his train set. Expect him to come barreling in here, talking nonstop, any minute now."

There was a moment. A little awkward. Too quiet. But somehow, with sparks.

Linc broke the silence. "They've had lunch."

"Terrific. So we're still on for Thanksgiving at Daniel's tomorrow?" She needed to ask. After last night, maybe he'd changed his mind about that.

"I'm looking forward to it," he replied.

She felt altogether too pleased at the news. "Great. I'll take the side-dish stuff home with me tonight."

"I appreciate this. Whatever cooking you have to do, consider it on the clock."

"No. It's Thanksgiving. I would be cooking anyway—except this year, my boss has covered the cost of all my ingredients. So thank you for that. I'm thinking we should leave about eleven or so tomorrow?"

"We'll come pick you up." He looked at her so steadily.

She imagined banked fires smoldering in his eyes. Like in those old romance novels where the men looked like Fabio and all the heroines had tumbling hair and heaving bosoms—and what were they talking about?

Focus, Harper. "Eleven, then." She made her tone brisk. "I'll be ready. As for today, I spoke with my sister and she's found slots for both kids in the show. So I would like to head over there now. I can get them started, introduce them around. Hailey and the other children will make them feel welcome. It will be fun. We should be back around five, if that works for you?"

"No problem. I've got no end of online meetings before everyone takes off for the long weekend. You think you can stay until bedtime tonight?"

"Of course." More hours. Excellent.

"About dinner…"

"I'll be happy to cook."

"I really hoped you would say that." He gave her one of those warm, grateful smiles—the kind that could so easily have her forgetting all the reasons the two of them would never be a thing.

She summoned her most businesslike tone. "No problem. As for today at the theater, Maya and I will be winging it." She met the little girl's eyes and they shared a smile. "If it doesn't work out for one reason or another, we can always come home and then go pick up Jayden later."

"Sounds good. Take the Range Rover. Keys are in the bowl there." As he spoke, his cell rang in his hand. "I need to get this..."

She had no business feeling dismissed—and yet somehow, she did. Probably because she barely knew him, and yet already, she wanted more from him than was wise, more than she could afford to let herself have. "All right, then. See you at five."

With a wave of his hand, he turned for the room he'd set up as an office, answering the call as he went. "This is Linc...Hi, David. Of course. Just heading into my office to switch to the laptop now..."

The afternoon at the theater worked out even better than Hailey had hoped. Jayden reconnected with kids he'd met last year and made some new friends.

Maya did great. Hailey's mother-in-law-to-be, Sasha Marek Holland, was there to help backstage. Sasha was amazing with the little ones. And between Sasha, Harper, Hailey and Hailey's assistant director, Rashonda Kyle, someone was always available to keep a close eye on Maya.

Harper and the kids were back at the cottage by five as promised. She made spaghetti with her favorite bottled sauce and cut up a salad to go with it. They sat down to eat at a little after six.

Too soon, it was seven thirty and she was tucking Jayden into his bed as Linc put Maya in her crib.

Downstairs, she saw that Linc's office door was shut. She gathered up the food she wanted to take to Daniel's tomorrow and then tapped on the office door.

Linc pulled it open. He had his cell phone in his hand.

"I'm out of here. I'll see you at eleven tomorrow." Did she hold out hope that he might try to coax her into spending a few minutes with him, decompressing a bit at the end of the day?

She most certainly did. Even if the expectation was completely unreasonable. Hadn't she made it painfully clear that they wouldn't be sharing wine by the fire again anytime soon?

He gave her a quick smile. "We'll be there, thanks." He put the phone to his ear as he shut the door.

Dismissed.

No doubt about it.

She returned to the kitchen to grab the bags of groceries and went home to her cottage, where she assembled a sweet potato casserole, made some cranberry relish and tried a new recipe for cheesy baked brussels sprouts. By the time she finished prepping the food, it was almost ten.

And she didn't feel the least bit tired.

She ended up in the living room, working on costumes for the Christmas show with *Little Women* on the flat-screen TV, trying not to feel sad and lonely. Practically everyone she knew was coupled up, leaving her on her own in the quiet cottage, wishing for things she couldn't allow herself to have.

It was after one when she finally went to bed. Sleep was elusive. She stared at the shadowed beadboard ceiling overhead and tried not to regret drawing the line on Linc the night before.

Linc and the kids arrived right on time the next day. He and Jayden helped carry the food she'd prepared to the Range Rover, and they set off for the house where Harper had grown up.

A big Colonial on several wooded acres perched atop Rhinehart Hill on the east side of town, the Bravo house was packed with Bravos and extended family. Jayden and Maya happily joined the other kids, of whom there were several now. They all trooped through the house in a pack, with the older ones leading the way, either carrying the little ones or making sure they didn't wander too far from the group.

Linc seemed relaxed, Harper thought. She introduced him to her ancient great-uncle Percy and her great-aunt Daffodil. He visited with her brothers and was cordial with her sisters. When Keely and Daniel's toddler, Marie, climbed up onto the sofa and cuddled up next to him, he moved his arm to the backrest so Marie could more easily lean against him and went right on talking salmon fishing with Harper's brother Liam.

"You *really* like that guy," Hailey whispered to her when they were alone for a moment in the kitchen, checking on the dinner rolls before the big push to get everything on the tables in the dining room.

"Not going there," she whispered under her breath.

Hailey only laughed. "I notice you're not even trying to deny that you're interested."

What was the point? Hailey would know she was lying.

So fine. She really liked him. A lot. He was not only yummy to look at, but he also seemed like a good person, someone who was honestly interested in others, in who they were and what made them tick. Megan had been the same way.

Harper watched him interacting with her family and wondered about his parents. They must be special, to have raised a son and a daughter like Linc and Megan. Strange that Linc's parents weren't here in town for the holidays. Linc had mentioned it was a family tradition to spend Christmas at the Stryker cottage.

Come to think of it, Linc's parents hadn't been here last year, either—well, not that she remembered, anyway. They'd probably dropped in on a day when Harper wasn't around.

The big meal went on for over an hour. There was a lot of food and the Bravos felt honor bound to do it justice.

They always took a break before dessert. Some of them put on their coats and sat out on the wide front porch, some strolled the garden paths in the backyard.

Harper checked on the kids. They seemed happy. Maya and little Marie were lying on the floor together, both of them staring dreamily up at the ceiling, chewing on teething toys. Liam's ten-year-old stepson, Ben Killigan, seemed to have taken Jayden under his wing. They sat near Marie and Maya. Ben was building something with wheels and gears from a metal construction set as Jayden peppered him with questions, each one of which Ben patiently answered.

Harper went looking for Linc—after all, he was her guest. She wanted him to be comfortable, to have a good time.

She found him out on the back porch with Hailey's fiancé, Roman. They were deep in conversation, talking real estate. Roman had a project he was developing in Portland. It sounded as though Linc might be considering an investment.

Did she imagine stepping up next to Linc and having him casually put his arm around her—like he was more than her boss, more than her guest for the afternoon?

Like she was someone special to him and he wanted her close?

Yeah, maybe.

So what? A girl had a right to a little fantasy now and then. Nothing would happen between them. She'd already made way too sure of that.

Feeling a little sad for no real reason, she went back inside to find her big brother Daniel lurking in the mudroom. He had that look—the one he got when someone in the family needed checking on.

Daniel took his duties as honorary family dad very seriously. "Hey. There you are. Got a minute?"

She wanted to be annoyed with him, but Daniel was a sweetheart, so steady and upstanding. It was hard to be mad at him. "Sure. Just don't make me drink scotch. Please." Daniel liked to take friends and family into his study at the front of the house and serve them top-shelf single malt to go with his honest concern for their success and well-being. "It's wasted on me, Daniel." *Like drinking peat moss*, she thought but had the grace not to say.

He grinned at that. "There will be options. This way…"

In her brother's study with the door closed, Harper took a seat on the leather sofa and accepted a small glass of local brandy. "Delicious," she said, after a first careful sip. "And okay. Consider me braced. You may proceed with the interrogation."

Daniel chuckled and sipped his scotch. She loved seeing him so happy. In the old days, he used to look like he carried the weight of the world on his shoulders. Not anymore, though. He'd raised seven of his siblings to successful adulthood. He loved his wife and his kids—little Marie, and the twins from his first marriage. These days, Daniel smiled a lot more than he used to.

"I just wanted to catch up with you," he said mildly. "How're you doing in the cottage now that Hailey's moved in with Roman?"

She answered honestly, "It can get a little lonely, but I'm managing." And now seemed as good a time as any to share her moving plans with him. "Actually, I've been meaning to tell you about what I want to do next year. I'm going to try a move to Seattle, look for something new workwise. Lee-Lee's on board with it. We'll miss each other, but it's time for me to try my wings, I guess you could say."

"You hope to find something with a theater company there?"

"Unlikely. I applied for a paid internship with an architectural firm up there a couple of months ago. It didn't come through, but it would have given me enough to live on. And that got me thinking that unless I want to move to New York or LA, a life in the theater may not be for me. I would rather stay a little closer to home."

"I can't help liking the idea of you staying nearby…"

"We'll see."

Daniel had a slow, thoughtful sip of his drink. "Linc Stryker seems like a fine man."

Had she known that was coming? Unfortunately, yes. "He really appreciated being invited to dinner. He was going to order takeout. Can you believe it?"

"Can't have that. I'm glad you talked him into coming. I spoke to him briefly, gave him my sympathies on the loss of his sister and her husband."

She decided to cut to the chase. "He's paying me a premium rate to help with the kids through the holidays. It's good for both of us. I save money toward my move, and he can work remotely in the afternoons."

"So it's just a job for you then?"

"Yes." Did she say that too strongly? Well, it never hurt to be crystal clear with Daniel. "I love the kids and I like to keep busy, so it's a win all the way around."

"You know I'm here, right?"

"I do, Daniel. Thank you."

"If the cottage is too lonely now—"

"It's not. I'm fine. I promise you."

He gave her a gentle smile. "I'm making you uncomfortable."

"Maybe. A little."

He set down his glass. She did the same. They rose simultaneously and shared a quick hug. "I'm proud of you, Harp."

She smiled up at him. "It means a lot, to hear you say that. Keep in mind, though, that while I appreciate any advice you give me, I'm going to do things my own way."

"I get that."

"And I…well, I do really like Linc."

"But…?"

She thought of Linc's ex-fiancée. A guy didn't get over a serious relationship in a week, and that was almost how long it had been since Linc's engagement had ended. "Truthfully, it's just bad timing, you know?"

"Because he's in Portland and you're moving to Seattle?"

She knew she'd said too much already—and yet, she just kept talking. "There's that, yes. And I *work* for him."

The gleam in her big brother's eye said it all. "Wouldn't that be shocking, you and Linc getting together? I mean, falling for the nanny. Who does that?"

"Omigod. I didn't even think of you and Keely…" Daniel and Keely had gotten together when Daniel had nanny troubles and Keely stepped in to take care of the twins.

Daniel nodded. "You never really know how things will work out. Be open to all the possibilities. That's all I'm saying."

Color her blown away. Never would she have imagined that Daniel would encourage her to give Linc Stryker a chance. As a rule, Daniel had the overprotective-big-brother act down pat. "I, um, yeah. Sure. Thanks, Daniel. I'll do that."

For the rest of the afternoon and into the early evening, Harper couldn't stop thinking about what Daniel had said.

"You want to go straight home?" Linc asked when they were on their way down the hill from Daniel's house.

From the back seat, Jayden objected, "Don't go home, Harper. I need you to tuck me in."

Linc sent her a wry glance. "You don't have to give in to a five-year-old's demands."

"I know. But it *is* Thanksgiving…" And who was she kidding? She didn't want to go home yet. She wanted to…be open to all the possibilities. Like her big brother had told her to do.

Jayden kept pushing. "Harper, *please*…"

Linc cut him off in a firm, level voice. "It's Harper's decision, Jayden."

A silence, then, so sweetly, "Sorry," from the back seat.

She and Linc shared another glance—more than friendly. Conspiratorial. Like they had secrets together.

A memory came to her. Of sitting in the back seat as a child before her parents died. It was dark out, same as now. Her mom sat in the passenger seat, her dad at the wheel. She remembered her parents turning to each other, sharing a glance, their faces in profile. She couldn't have been more than six or seven, and she had no awareness of who else was in the car at the time. What she did have, right now, was the achingly clear sense that her parents spoke to each other without saying a word.

In that moment, she'd felt such peace, firmly strapped in the back seat, her parents in front, leading the way, solid with each other, invincible together, keeping her safe…

Swallowing down the knot of emotion that had lodged in her throat, Harper said, "I think I'll go to your place first, if that works for you?"

Linc glanced her way yet again, his eyes warm, the cool, careful distance of yesterday vanished as though it had never been. "Works for me."

Like night-before-last, Linc stood at the foot of the stairs when she came down from saying goodnight to Jayden. He was heartbreaker-handsome in his gray dress pants and a beautiful cream-colored sweater. "Thank you," he said. "For today. The kids loved it. I did, too."

"I'm glad you were there."

He glanced away and then back, his expression a little wary, but also determined. "I shouldn't ask…"

She couldn't hide her smile—and she didn't even try. "Yes, you should."

"Stay. Just for a little while…"

"I'd like that, yes."

"I was thinking hot chocolate, for some reason…"

"I'm in. Let's see what we have to work with."

He followed her to the kitchen, where they found milk, cocoa, sugar and vanilla—but no marshmallows. She made a mental note to add them to her shopping list.

"Here we go," she said as she raided the spice rack. "Cinnamon sticks and cayenne."

He stood at the end of the counter, looking puzzled. "Cayenne pepper?"

"Just a pinch or two. It's my secret ingredient. You're gonna love it."

Ten minutes later, they sat on the sofa in front of the fire.

"It's really good," he said after the first sip.

"Thanks. I miss the marshmallows, but still. Hot cocoa is a perfect choice on a chilly night—with or without the white fluffy goodness."

He watched her so closely, she started to wonder if she had cocoa powder on her nose. But then he said, "It's another sad milestone, you know? First Thanksgiving without them…"

"Yeah." The word escaped her in a near whisper. "The whole first year is rough."

"You're telling me that it gets better?"

"I know it's not news, but yeah." She bent forward to set down her mug. "It does."

He put his mug beside hers and then leaned back.

"I kind of set myself up for disaster with all this," he said.

"Not following. All this?"

One thick, hard shoulder lifted in a shrug. "Bringing Jayden and Maya here for Christmas at the cottage, but minus anything resembling reasonable preparation. I keep messing up. And then, there you are, saving my ass yet again. Today could have been awful, me and the kids with whatever takeout I could scrounge up..." He turned more fully toward her, bracing an elbow on the back of the sofa.

She mirrored his pose. "Stop beating yourself up. You're doing great."

He leaned a little closer. That worked for her. He smelled so good, and she couldn't get enough of the sweet things he said. "I love those dimples you have—" he brushed a touch against one cheek and then the other, causing heat to sear across her skin "—when you smile." He caught a lock of her hair and rubbed it between his fingers. "So soft..."

She leaned closer, too, into the moment, into the scent of him—cinnamon and chocolate and man. His mouth was so tempting and full, his eyes darker than before, mysteriously shadowed with tender intent.

And then he did just what she needed him to do. He leaned that all-important fraction closer and his lips were touching hers, brushing so lightly, tasting of hot cocoa with a hint of cayenne. With a happy sigh, she pressed closer.

He gathered her in, his mouth opening over hers, his teeth nipping just a little. She gave way to him gladly, letting him in with a small, throaty moan.

His arms tightened around her. They felt just right, big and strong and encompassing. She surrendered—to his touch, to the feel of his muscled chest against her soft breasts, to the wonder of those lean hands at her back.

The kiss went deeper. Lost in sweet sensation, she lay back, pulling him down on top of her across the sofa.

He was heavy and warm. His mouth felt so good pressed to hers. So good and so right.

Should there be warning bells going off in her head?

Probably.

Eighty bucks an hour was nothing to sneeze at. When the kissing was over, she could easily lose a major addition to her relocation fund.

But somehow, at this moment, a fat paycheck meant nothing.

The feel of this—his body on top of her, pressing her down, his full lips moving on hers, the taste of him in her mouth…

This intimacy, this connection with him.

It was everything, all the things she always tried not to let herself admit she'd been missing.

She might have, just maybe, started to wonder if there was something somehow lacking in her. Everybody else she knew seemed to be finding the hot magic, coupling up and reveling in it.

Like dominoes, they fell in an endless chain, to passion and excitement and love ever after—and okay, maybe she was getting a little carried away here. It was only kissing.

Thoroughly excellent, delicious, fabulous and overwhelming kissing.

But just kissing, nonetheless.

Just really good kissing and she wanted more of it.

Linc's big body covered hers so perfectly, and his mouth made love to hers and it was fireworks and a brass band, Christmas and New Year's and every good thing all wrapped up in his lips on her lips and his body touching hers.

Until, with no warning, he ripped his mouth from hers.

"Don't..." She grabbed for him to keep him there, but he braced his hands on either side of her and pushed himself back even more. Dazed and yearning, she blinked up at him.

His mouth was swollen from kissing her, his face flushed crimson. His thick hair looked wild, as if he'd been set upon by hurricane-force winds. She must have been clutching fistfuls of it. "I shouldn't have done that," he said.

She felt a hot stab of guilt. Was this about the ex-fiancée, somehow? Did he still love her and consider kissing someone else a betrayal of that love?

But why? That was over, right? He'd said so. He wasn't with anyone and neither was she.

She gaped up at him in complete disbelief. "Um, what just happened?"

He sat up and raked his fingers through all that scrambled hair, smoothing it down. And then he shook his head at her, his beautiful eyes full of regret. "This is all kinds of wrong. We went over all this the other night. You *work* for me and here I am, taking advantage of you…"

Tugging on her silk shirt that had somehow gotten all twisted around in the excitement, she scrambled to a sitting position, too, scooting back from him until her butt hit the sofa arm. "Really, Linc? Harassment? You're going to go there?"

He looked very noble, sitting so straight, his square jaw determined, his beautiful sexy mouth set. "It's a bad idea."

She knew exactly what he meant, but she asked, anyway, "What is?"

"This—us. I can't believe I just kissed you."

A girl could only take so much. She threw up both hands. "No problem," she replied sweetly. "I quit."

Now he looked kind of terrified, and she couldn't help feeling gratified about that. "Please." He put up both hands. "Don't quit, Harper. Don't do that."

Rising, she tucked in her shirt and shoved her wildly tangled hair out of her eyes. It was definitely time to call it a night. "I do not work for Stryker Marine Transport. I'm an independent contractor and you are in no way harassing me. If you were, frankly, you wouldn't be so concerned about it—but you know what? Enough. Happy Thanksgiving. And good night, Linc."

She headed for the door.

Chapter Four

Linc watched her go. Through a supreme effort of will, he did not call her back or leap up and run after her.

Oh, but he wanted to.

He heard the front door open and then shut. She was gone.

And he had no idea if he would ever see her again.

He'd messed up so bad. Two nights ago, they'd agreed to keep it cool and professional.

And then tonight…

He really shouldn't have done that, shouldn't have pushed her down and crawled on top of her and let himself get swept away in the feel of her, the scent of her, the perfection of her sweet, curvy body in his arms.

It was wrong.

Wasn't it?

God.

It hadn't *felt* wrong. On the contrary, kissing Harper Bravo had felt right in a way that not a lot in his life ever had.

Had she really quit? He didn't want her to quit. He missed her already, and she'd just walked out the door.

And what about the kids? He didn't know how he was going to explain her absence to the kids. They would be hurt that she hadn't even said goodbye.

No.

Wait.

She couldn't have quit. Harper wouldn't do that to Maya and Jayden.

She'd been yanking his chain.

Hadn't she?

It was all way too damn confusing.

For a while, he just sat there by the fire and indulged in deep thoughts about his life and his choices.

He thought of his sister, of how he hadn't spent enough time with her in the past decade or so— since their dad dumped their mom and married his twenty-eight-year-old assistant at Stryker Marine, followed quickly by their mom setting out, as she had put it, "in search of meaning." Alicia Stryker had become a globe-trotter for a while. Recently, she seemed to have settled in a villa in Tuscany. She pretty much never came home to Oregon anymore.

A few years after leaving his mom, Linc's dad had retired. Linc, young and untried, took over at Stryker Marine. The demanding work had given him yet more excuses for not spending time with his sister and her family. As for Linc's dad, Warren Stryker was now on his third wife, a woman younger than either of his children.

Linc thought how there were always reasons not to do the things a man most needed and wanted to do.

Now Megan and Kevin were gone. He could never tell them he was sorry for all the time they hadn't spent together, all the summer barbecues he'd missed, all the Thanksgiving dinners when he should have shared their table, all the Christmases here at the cottage, the ones he'd been too busy to show up for.

It all went in a circle, really. Bad choices created plenty of opportunities to make more bad choices.

Which led him back around to kissing Harper.

He was all over the damn map with her—desperate for a chance with her one minute, angry at himself for kissing her the next. Which was the bad choice?

The more he sat there and stared at the fire, the more he found himself thinking that the bad choice had been to *stop* kissing her...

* * *

Linc didn't get a lot of sleep that night.

Sometime after three, he finally drifted off. It seemed he'd just shut his eyes when he heard knocking on the bedroom door.

Jayden called out, "Uncle Linc, it's morning! Can we have pancakes and then go get our tree?"

The knocking and happy shouting woke Maya. On the nightstand, the baby monitor erupted with the sounds of her fussing.

"Uncle Linc, you know what?" Jayden called through the shut door.

"What, Jayden?"

"We should have *blueberry* pancakes. I really like them!"

Linc groaned and plopped his pillow over his head—but only for a second or two. Then he tossed the pillow aside and called, "Come on in, Jayden. The door's open..."

At which point, Maya cried, "Unc Winc, I wet!"

And that had him worrying about potty training. Should he be on that with Maya by now? Had Jean left him a note about it on the list of how-tos that he still hadn't found?

Didn't matter, Linc decided. His niece would hardly be damaged for life if she didn't start potty training until the new nanny he planned to hire when they returned to Portland came on board in January.

And just thinking the word *nanny* had his mind

circling back to last night and what had happened with Harper.

In his measly few hours of restless sleep, he'd come to a decision. If she didn't show today, he would track her down and get things worked out with her. Whatever she wanted, he would provide it.

More kisses? Definitely.

Strict respect for the accepted boundaries between boss and employee? Of course, if those were her terms.

A raise?

Sure, why not?

Jayden pushed the door open enough to stick his face in. Why did kids always look so happy and wide-awake in the morning? "Maya wants you."

He shoved back the covers and grabbed for the pair of sweats he'd thrown across the bedside chair.

The diaper change took a while. Jayden wanted to help and that seemed like a good thing, but during the process, Maya peed some more, which horrified Jayden—at first. The look on his little face was so comical, Linc let out a snort of laughter. And Jayden thought *that* was funny, so he started laughing, too.

Maya lay on the changing table, kicking her fat little legs, staring up at them as she chewed on her blue teething toy. After a few seconds, she seemed to decide that if the guys were laughing, then fine with her. She pulled her blue toy from her mouth and chortled right along with them.

Eventually they all settled down. Linc cleaned

up Maya and laid her on a fresh diaper. He showed Jayden how to position the tabs—not too tight and not too loose. Then he put Maya in her favorite pink fleece pants with the pink fleece top and the Minnie Mouse trim. Jayden helped with her pink socks and little white shoes.

Once she was fully dressed, Linc scooped her up, kissed her forehead and set her on her feet as Jayden pushed the chair he'd been standing on back under the kid-sized table in the middle of Maya's room.

They all three went downstairs to the kitchen, where Jayden headed straight to the freezer drawer.

"We got blueberries, Uncle Linc!" he crowed, holding the bag high.

"Excellent," Linc replied as he put Maya in her booster seat. He probably shouldn't be surprised about the blueberries. Harper had done the shopping, after all, and Harper thought of everything.

"Miwk, pwease?" asked Maya.

"You got it." Linc gave her a sippy cup of milk and some dry cereal to keep her busy while he got the pancakes going.

As usual, Jayden wanted to help. He stood on a step stool and poured the ingredients into the mixing bowl after Linc had measured out the right amounts of everything.

After mixing the batter, Linc put the dishes and flatware on the table and asked Jayden to set the places. Linc got busy at the griddle. He was flipping the first batch when he thought he heard a noise in the front hall.

Glancing that way, he saw Harper standing in the open arch that led back to the front door. He was so happy to see her, he almost flipped a pancake over his shoulder.

"Harper!" cried Jayden as Maya called, "Hawp!"

"Hey, guys. What's cookin'?"

Jayden launched right into how there were pancakes and he'd found the blueberries and he couldn't wait to go get the tree. In the meantime, Maya waved her sippy cup and brandished a fistful of cereal.

Jayden collected more flatware from a drawer and set a place for her as Harper took a couple of juice boxes from the fridge, putting one at Jayden's place and offering Maya the other. The little girl handed over her empty sippy cup in exchange.

Linc became so absorbed in watching them, he almost burned the pancakes, but got them off the griddle and onto the serving platter just as Harper came toward him again. She stopped a few feet from him to pour herself a cup of coffee from the coffee maker on the counter near the cooktop. Their eyes met. She gave him a devilish smile, and he almost dropped the plate of pancakes.

"Nothing going on at the theater today," she said. "Thought I'd come early." She set down the pot, picked up her mug and had a slow sip. "If that's all right…"

He couldn't agree fast enough. "Yeah. All morning, all afternoon and into the evening." The words came out low and rough, though he'd meant to sound easy and carefree. "We really need you today. There will be lots of overtime."

Harper tried not to grin too widely. Last night had been awkward, but this morning he talked about overtime. It could have been worse.

"I love overtime," she said. "Here. Give me that."

He passed her the platter. She carried it to the table and began helping the kids with butter and syrup and cutting the pancakes into bite-size bits.

It had been a cold night—no snow, but frost glittered on the porch railings and rooftops. After breakfast, they headed out to find the right tree. Harper knew the best tree farm. By eleven, they were strapping a gorgeous, thick Fraser fir onto the rack atop the Range Rover.

Back at the house, they brought it in and put it in the stand in front of one of the big windows in the living area. Jayden stood awestruck, gazing up at it, declaring, "It's even bigger than last year!"

After a break for sandwiches and chicken noodle soup, Maya took a nap. Jayden, Linc and Harper trooped down into the storage area off the garage to bring up the endless boxes of decorations stacked under the house over the past thirty-plus years of Stryker and Hollister family Christmases.

Maya woke up after an hour or so and Harper brought her out to join the fun. The afternoon was spent decorating. In addition to the tree, there were snow scenes, a manger scene and a lot of fake greenery. Fat candles, shiny balls and lights had to be arranged on the mantel and on various tables and sideboards.

By late afternoon, Maya was content to lie on the floor. With her chew toy in one hand and Pebble cuddled close in the other, she stared up, wide-eyed, at all the lights and bright decorations.

Jayden was hyped. "Wait! We have to do the outside lights before it gets too dark."

"The handyman is going to put those up tomorrow," Linc said.

Jayden did not approve. "But the handyman isn't *family* and it is only *family* at the cottage."

Linc crouched down and gave Jayden's shoulder a squeeze. "We're making an exception in this case. The way we did for Harper."

Jayden was doubtful. "Is he a *nice* handyman?"

"Well, I haven't met him yet, but he has excellent references."

"What's 'references'?"

"References are when other people someone has worked for say he's a good worker and you can depend on him."

"Hmm." Jayden remained unconvinced. "What's his name?"

"Angus McTerly."

Harper knew she should probably stay out of it, but she stuck her nose in anyway. "I know Angus.

He lives nearby, two cottages south of my cottage. He is *genuinely nice*. And he has a friendly dog named Mitsy."

Jayden folded his arms across his little chest and pondered that information. "I like dogs. Will he *bring* the dog named Mitsy?"

Linc caught Harper's eye. She read his expression. It said, *Your move. Make it good.*

She smirked at him and then suggested to Jayden, "I'll call him and ask him to bring Mitsy along."

"Okay." Mitsy had tipped the scales for Jayden. "The handyman can put up the outside lights this year and bring Mitsy."

"Excellent." Linc rose.

"Uncle Linc?" Jayden stared up at his uncle hopefully. "I've been thinking. I *really* want a puppy for Christmas." Linc frowned. Jayden, as usual, just kept on talking. "And that 'minds me. I need to write my letter to Santa. You and Harper can help and then you can help me write one for Maya, too."

"One Christmas project at a time," Linc replied. "Today we did a lot. Let's save the letters for another day."

"Tomorrow? Please?"

"Sure. Tomorrow."

"And what about a puppy? Can I have a puppy?"

Linc kept his mouth shut and gazed down at his nephew patiently.

As for Jayden, he was a very bright boy who

knew when *not* to push his luck. "Maybe you could just think about the puppy, Uncle Linc?"

"I'll do that."

"O-*kay*!"

Linc paused. "You know what, Jayden?"

The boy wrinkled his button nose. "What?"

"*If* we do get you a puppy, it will be next year, after we're back home in Portland."

Jayden stuck out his lower lip. "No puppy for Christmas?"

"Sorry. No puppy for Christmas."

"But maybe sometime later?"

"We'll see."

Jayden seemed to realize that was as far as he was getting on the puppy question today. His "okay" wasn't quite as enthusiastic as before, but he gave a little nod with it that seemed to say he'd accepted Linc's decision.

On the floor nearby, Maya took her chew toy out of her mouth. "I hungwy," she announced to no one in particular.

Harper bent and scooped her up. "Let's head on into the kitchen and see what we can do about that…"

For the rest of the afternoon and evening, both kids were fussy, which was no surprise to Harper. All the excitement had exhausted them.

But when Harper mentioned bedtime, both of them objected.

Maya stuck her lip out. "No. No bed."

Jayden argued, "It's still early."

Harper and Linc tacitly decided not to fight them on it.

Five minutes later, for no discernable reason, Maya started crying and wouldn't stop. Jayden complained that she hurt his ears and couldn't they make her be quiet, please?

Then, in the middle of a long, sad wail, Maya dropped to her bottom on the floor, toppled to her side and went to sleep.

Harper bent down and felt her forehead, just in case. "No fever. I think she's just worn out."

Linc carried the little girl upstairs to get her ready for bed while Harper herded Jayden up there, as well. The boy spent a good half hour in the bathroom washing his face and brushing his teeth, after which he announced he would read to Harper—meaning he would choose a book he had pretty much memorized and "read" it by turning the pages and telling it from memory.

Harper cuddled up with him on his Star Wars quilt and Jayden began "reading" her the *Me and My Dragon* Christmas book.

Linc stuck his head in the door and mouthed, "Wine?"

She probably shouldn't. Wine was dangerous. Then again, last night they'd only had cocoa and look what had happened. Maybe their chemistry was just too powerful to ignore. She gave him a nod.

Why not? She deserved a nice glass of red and a hot guy to drink it with.

"Uncle Linc, come let me read you a story," Jayden commanded. "It's the one about the dragon and the Christmas spirit."

"Can't miss that." Linc joined them, circling around to Jayden's other side. It was kind of a tight fit, the three of them on the single bed, but Jayden looked pleased as he continued with the story of the little boy who taught his dragon all about what Christmas really means.

When he closed the book, Harper suggested that maybe he would like his uncle to tuck him in tonight. Jayden agreed that he would like that a lot, and Harper left them to it.

She was in the kitchen putting the last of the dishes in the dishwasher and tidying up when Linc joined her.

"How about champagne tonight?" he offered.

"Feeling festive?"

"Hey. We decorated the tree today. That's something to celebrate." His eyes got softer, more gold than brown. "And you came back."

"Linc." She dropped the sponge in the sink and moved a few steps in his direction. "I was only joking about quitting."

"Good."

She'd reached the marble-topped island, and he was near the fridge by then, almost close enough to touch. "I *was* annoyed with you."

"Yeah." He glanced down and then back up into her waiting eyes. "Got that." Energy seemed to vibrate in the air between them, an electric feeling, impossible to ignore.

She admitted, "I, um, felt a little guilty for being so hard on you. I know you were only trying to do the right thing."

He looked solemn suddenly. "I was, yes."

"I actually researched the harassment question last night, when I got home."

"You did?" Now he seemed cautious. "So then, you *do* think I was harassing you?"

She exerted great effort *not* to roll her eyes. "No. I was interested, so I looked it up online."

"Ah." He gave her a slow, wary nod.

"I learned that sexual harassment really is a particularly bad problem for housekeepers and nannies. It's different, working in the home where the employer lives. Domestic workers aren't formally covered by the same laws that protect most employees."

He watched her steadily now. "At Stryker Marine, the employee manual has a whole section on harassment. Anyone in a supervisory capacity is required to take an online course so we know they understand what is and is not harassment."

"And you're telling me that you took that course?"

"Yes, I did."

"But, Linc, you really weren't harassing me."

He put up both hands. "There's no need to go on and on about this."

"I'm not. I'm only trying to clear the air, you know? And what I'm getting at is that it's still about consent. *If* we ended up in bed together, it wouldn't be harassment because I can promise you, I would not go to bed with you unless I wanted to be there. Are we perfectly clear?"

"We are, yes. So very painfully clear." He looked more than a little uneasy. The muscles in his arm flexed beneath his snug sweater as he rubbed the back of his neck. "So what, exactly, is happening here?"

Was she giving him a headache?

Probably.

But she'd come this far. Might as well drill her point home. "We are coming to an understanding on the harassment question—meaning that there isn't any in our situation. And now that we've got that settled, we are tabling this discussion."

He seemed more confused than ever—and a little unsure as to whether he should allow himself to look directly at her. "Harper, I'm not completely clear as to what you're telling me. Are you still the nanny?"

"Do you *want* me to still be the nanny?"

"God, yes."

"And I need the money. So okay, then. I didn't really quit, and you don't want me to quit."

He shook his head and then he nodded. "Works for me."

"And I've made you uncomfortable, haven't I?"

"Yeah, kind of. But I'll get over it." He arched a sable eyebrow. "Champagne?"

She longed to say yes. But she'd made too big a deal about the harassment thing and now it was awkward between them. She needed to keep her feet on the ground here, to remember that, while she might feel sometimes that they were close and growing closer, they weren't.

They had a very temporary and practical arrangement. She needed to remember that she really didn't know him. He'd been engaged way too recently and acting on her attraction to him was a bad idea. When the holiday season was over, they would be headed in different directions.

"So, then." He was watching her, more wary than ever. "That's a no on the champagne?"

"Yeah, I think I'd better pass—and tomorrow's Saturday. I thought I would go with our original plan and take weekends off?"

"Of course." Did he look surprised? Upset?

Why wouldn't he be—on both counts? She'd handled this whole conversation with all the finesse of a toddler about to throw a tantrum. Probably by now he just wished she would shut up and leave. "I can get a lot done at the theater if I can work straight through a couple of days in a row."

"I understand. No problem."

"Well, okay then. See you Monday, around one?" She stared at him, waiting for… What?

There was nothing else to say.

With a plastered-on smile and a quick nod, she turned for the arch that led to the front door.

"I'm thinking these for the angels' robes…" Harper held up a stack of old white sheets. She and Hailey were downtown at the Pacific Bargain Mall, scouting props and costume materials for the Christmas show. "They're soft from years of washing, which means they'll be comfortable to wear and easy to handle. We'll just cut and fold and hem them at the neck hole. I've got a bunch of those gold graduation honor cords we can use as a tie at the waist. And gold foil on the wings and for the halos, I think. It's simpler and also showier from the stage than trying to do feathers…"

"Sounds good." Hailey paused. "Look at me."

Harper met her eyes. "What?"

"What's wrong?"

"Huh? Nothing."

"Liar." Hailey grabbed her arm. "Buy the sheets and let's go get a coffee."

Ten minutes later they had white chocolate peppermint mochas and a corner table at the Steamy Bean, which wasn't far from the Bargain Mall. John Legend crooned "By Christmas Eve" from a speaker above the espresso machine. Outside, the sky was gray and overcast, but evergreen wreaths hung from the streetlamps. Across the street, the Salvation Army bell ringer stood by her red kettle in front of the bookstore.

Hailey licked the whipped-cream mustache from her upper lip. "Is it the move? You're nervous about how it's going to work out?"

"Yeah. No. I don't know…"

"Well, that's specific." Hailey put her hand over Harper's. "I'll miss you so bad."

"And I'll miss you."

"But, Harp, it's the right decision for you. And I'll come with you when you go, stay with you in Seattle until we find you a good place and you're all settled in."

"You're the best." Harper turned her hand over and gave her sister's fingers a squeeze. "But it's not really the move."

"Hmm. Must be the guy, then."

"I have no idea what you're talking about."

Hailey scoffed. "Stop. It's not like I can't read your mind."

Harper covered her face with both hands and let out a groan. "I like him. I like him too much and I'm acting weird with him and… I don't know. It's like I'm thirteen again with a hopeless crush on Deacon Marsh."

Hailey grinned. "Wow. Deacon Marsh. Yeah, that didn't go well." Deacon was three years older than Harper. He'd played drums in a garage band and had zero interest in the skinny eighth grader with braces.

"I followed him everywhere." She put her face in her hands again. "He was always dismissing me, growling at me to get lost. It was so painful."

Hailey gave Harper's arm a comforting stroke. "I know. I remember." She sat back and had another sip of her peppermint mocha—a slow and contemplative one. "But you got over him."

"Yeah. One day, I woke up and…my heart no longer yearned for Deacon. I started going out with Brad Joiner."

"You notice how you always sound so blah about Brad?"

"Because I am blah about Brad—and I was blah at the time. I liked Brad. But he was no Deacon." She picked up her spoon and poked at the whipped cream on her coffee. "There was never that thrill just at the thought of him, never the burning need to see him, be near him, to get him to smile at me…" Glancing up, she met her sister's eyes.

"Enough about Brad. What happened with Linc?"

"Thanksgiving night…"

Hailey leaned in again. "I knew it. Things got cozy, didn't they?"

"We had hot chocolate by the fire after the kids were in bed. There was kissing. He stopped it and then apologized for taking advantage of me."

"*Was* he taking advantage of you?"

"No. But now it's awkward. *I'm* awkward. I'm thinking that I haven't felt this way since Deacon Marsh, that I've never had a boyfriend who thrills me, you know? I pick the blah boyfriends and I have the occasional fun, easygoing hookup. And my lack of experience in all the big, passionate emotions only makes me feel worse about the whole situation."

"So…you've got that thrill with Linc. You've got the burning need."

"Well, that just sounds ridiculous."

"No. It sounds like you *really* like Linc Stryker. And there is nothing wrong with that. I mean, come on. What's the worst that can happen?"

"He'll tell me it's gotten too weird and awkward. He'll tell me to get lost—in a kind and gentle way, and I'll lose several thousand bucks that I can put to good use in February."

"Meh."

"Seriously? You're meh-ing me?"

"Yes, I am. You weren't counting on that job before you got it. I know you've got savings and at least half of your inheritance left." The Bravos had all received some family money at the age of eighteen. "And then there's Valentine Logging." They all owned shares in the family business, which paid modest quarterly dividends. "And if all else fails, you can get money from Aunt Daffy or Uncle Percy or Daniel or Liam—and hey. There's also Roman. He's got plenty. I'm happy to hit him up for you if you need it."

Harper snort-laughed. "I do not need to go scrounging funds from the people I care about."

"My point exactly. You'll manage with or without this nanny job—though I do love the Hollister kids, and you're really good with them. That would be kind of sad, if they lost you. But then again, they're losing you at the first of the year, anyway."

"Okay, now you're just making *me* sad."

"You *want* to be sad. And conflicted. You need to stop with the whining and go after the hot CEO from Portland."

"But…"

Hailey waived a dismissing hand. "But what?"

"I have reasons."

"Of course, you do."

Harper glared at her sister. "*Good* reasons."

"Like what?"

"Well, he was engaged until a week ago yesterday."

"Is he engaged now?" Hailey immediately proceeded to answer her own question. "No, he is not. You need to enjoy your time with Jayden and Maya and let things happen with Linc if they're going to happen. Get out of your own way, Harp. Be open to…possibilities."

"Now you sound like Daniel," Harper muttered.

"What's Daniel got to do with this?"

"He took me aside at Thanksgiving. He likes Linc and he picked up on the attraction between us. He just wanted to encourage me to be open to whatever might happen with Linc."

Hailey reached across the table and tugged on Harper's single braid. "You are amazing and powerful and don't you forget it. And Daniel is right. Whatever happens in life, a woman should never miss the chance to get with the guy who has her burning and yearning."

"What if he breaks my heart?"

"What if he doesn't? What if he's as crazy about you as you are about him? What if this is the guy for you and you're too busy with all your thousand reasons why it can't work with him to relax and give him a chance? What if you lose him and then you meet another Brad or a second Kent and you settle?" Kent was her boyfriend at UO. "You're not a settler, Harp."

Hailey's voice had grown louder as she made her point. "If you settle for some guy who doesn't ring all your bells, you'll never find the happiness you deserve, and I think you know that. You've got to put yourself out there, open your heart, make yourself available for all the good things to be yours. Fortune favors the bold and she who hesitates is screwed and don't you forget it!" Hailey pounded the table for emphasis. Their mochas jumped.

They stared at each other, realizing simultaneously that it was suddenly way too quiet in the Steamy Bean.

And then the two baristas started clapping. The three women at the next table joined in. A guy by the window whistled and stomped his feet.

Ever the diva, Hailey got up and took a bow.

Chapter Five

When Harper let herself in the front door of the Stryker cottage Monday afternoon, silence greeted her. "Anybody home?"

Nobody answered.

But from the foyer, she could see that the tree was lit up in the living area. They all must be upstairs or maybe in the office. She swallowed down the nervousness that came from not quite knowing how Linc would greet her after the way they'd left things Friday night. Every time she thought about that, she cringed. She'd lectured him and turned down the wine she'd previously said yes to—and then raced out the door.

Really, she could hardly blame him if he found

ways to avoid too much contact with her now. And the more she thought about it, the more she worried he might be rethinking the wisdom of keeping her around at all.

Welp. No time like the present to find out.

She hung her coat on the rack by the door, dropped her tote on the hall table and went on into the living area, where the beautiful tree, ablaze with lights, stood in the window and the fire burned bright. She was about to detour to the kitchen when she spotted the trifold brochure on the coffee table.

Intrigued, she picked it up. The front had a company name, Acevedo Hybrid Homes, in a bold font, surrounded by color photos of modern-looking, boxy houses, with lots of windows and an interesting industrial feel.

She recognized those houses. They were increasingly popular all over the country. There was even a show about them on HGTV—*Container Homes*.

Made from retired shipping containers, the houses were sturdy and affordable. You could use them to create a tiny, eco-friendly, low-cost home with a modest footprint. You could also go big, find interesting ways to link them together, construct a shipping container mansion or even a whole apartment complex.

Was Linc considering building a container house? Or maybe investing in this company, Acevedo Hybrid Homes?

With a shrug, she dropped the brochure back on

the table where she'd found it and turned for the kitchen.

That was when she heard a tiny giggle, followed by Jayden whispering, "Shh. She'll hear us."

The sounds were coming from over by the tree. As she watched, the branches shook and ornaments clinked together.

She put a hand to her ear and asked, "What do I hear? It sounds like there might be elves behind the Christmas tree."

Another giggle, followed by more whispering— and then by both kids crawling out from behind the tree.

"Harper!" Jayden shouted, jumping up. "It's us!" He came running.

"Hawp!" It took Maya longer to get upright.

She managed it just as Jayden reached Harper. "We missed you!" he declared, gazing up at her with a giant smile of greeting. "You've been gone for two whole days."

"I missed you, too. But I'm back now." She dropped to a crouch to gather them both in just as Linc's tall, broad form unfolded from behind the recliner not far from the sofa.

"Surprise," he said a little sheepishly.

She hugged her two favorite "elves" and grinned like a long-gone fool at the handsome man by the fireplace.

"Hawp, Hawp!" Maya caught Harper's face between her little hands. "Hi!"

"Hi, sweetheart. It's so good to see you."

As usual, Jayden had questions. "Harper, are we going to go to practice for the Christmas show today?"

"Yes, we are."

"Are we going now?"

"Very soon. Did you have lunch?"

"Yes, we did!"

"Up!" Maya commanded. Harper gathered her close and stood.

Linc came toward them. He wore a steel blue thermal shirt that hugged his big arms and broad chest. His smile was so warm, like he'd been waiting forever for her to walk back in his door. All her apprehensions about seeing him again seemed kind of silly now that they stood face-to-face.

"Good weekend?" he asked.

She beamed up at him. "Very productive, yes. You?"

"Changed a lot of diapers, helped build a blanket fort and went camping right here in the living room in that bare spot in front of the tree."

"Sounds like fun."

Maya lifted her head from Harper's shoulder to announce, "Fun!"

"It was!" agreed Jayden.

Linc said, "And I haven't even mentioned that we wrote letters to Santa."

"Mine was really *long*," added Jayden, looking up at her eagerly.

Harper grinned down at him. "Did Angus and Mitsy come by?"

"Yes, they did!" Jayden replied. "I really like Mitsy and I *really* want a puppy, but I promised not to keep asking for one. And the lights outside look bee-u-tiful. Wait till it's dark. You'll see what I mean."

Linc nodded. "It's true about the lights. Angus did a fine job."

"And we made cookies," Jayden added. "They're sugar cookies, Harper. But they're kind of *hard*…"

"You're in for a treat," Linc said with a definite note of irony. "And I'm getting pretty tired of my own cooking. I was kind of hoping that you might be willing to stay late this evening?"

"To cook dinner, you mean?"

"Please." He put his hands together, prayer-fashion, and tapped the tips of his long fingers against that mouth she couldn't keep herself from hoping she might get to kiss again. "I am begging you." His voice was crushed velvet and that look in his eyes…

No doubt about it. If he'd been upset with her when she left Friday night, he'd gotten over it.

She gave him a slow, teasing smile. "Love that overtime."

"I was hoping you would say that."

She laughed. "I'll bet you have work to do."

"It's piling up, yeah. But my priority is right here in this living room." Why did she feel he meant her, in addition to his adorable nephew and niece? Oh, the guy was dangerous. In the best kind of way. "I mean it," he insisted. "Whatever you need my help with, I'm on it."

"Go," she said. "Work."

"You sure?"

Jayden's small fingers closed around her free hand. "Yeah, Uncle Linc. You can go. Harper's here. We have things we need to do."

That night, when she came down from tucking Jayden in, she found Linc in the kitchen.

They had a moment—her in the doorway, him by the counter, neither quite sure what to do or say next.

Harper remembered her sister's strong words. *Fortune favors the bold.* "It's been a long day. I'll take that champagne tonight—if the offer's still open."

He stepped away from the counter as she fully entered the room. They met by the island and then just stood there, grinning at each other. Her heart felt so light, like she might just float up to the gorgeous coffered cedar ceiling overhead.

"Champagne it is," he said.

"After all, it's Monday."

"You're right. There should always be bubbly on Monday."

She got down the glasses and he popped the cork. They went on into the living area to enjoy the tree and the fire.

Should she bring up the awkwardness last Friday night?

She was trying to decide whether to get into that when he said, "I have to tell you, I was kind of worried I'd blown it. Every time my phone rang over the weekend, I just knew it would be you, calling to say you weren't coming back."

She had a sip of fizzy wonderfulness. "I was afraid I had totally turned you off with my treatise on harassment."

He leaned a little closer. She could smell that wonderful cologne of his, woodsy and spicy and no doubt quite spendy. "Share your thoughts with me anytime." He tapped his glass to hers.

"You're sure about that?"

"Anything. I mean it. It might get awkward—"

"And weird?"

He chuckled, the sound low and manly, stirring a promise of desire. "Yeah, that, too. But I kind of like the way you think. I appreciate that you say what's on your mind."

"All right, then. Here's to speaking the truth." They touched flutes again. She sat back for a slow sip and her gaze fell on the brochure that was still on the coffee table. "So…considering building a container home?"

He looked flummoxed for a second, but then he followed her gaze. "You mean this?" He picked up the brochure. At her nod, he dropped it back on the table. "The Acevedos are a husband-and-wife team.

It's a small start-up. Mia designs the houses. Sam runs the builds. They've been after me for a while to give them regular access to our used containers at a price that's lower than we ordinarily get for them."

"Why would you do that—I mean, if you can sell them for more?"

"I like what I know of the Acevedos. Mia's a creative designer, and Sam's a good builder—brings it in on time and on budget. They've built a couple of large, beautiful container homes for people I know who love what they did for them. But they're not only in it to make it big. They're hooked up with Homes for the Homeless, too. They build a couple of houses a year for them." Like Habitat for Humanity, Homes for the Homeless built housing for people with limited incomes. "It's important—you know, to give back."

She wanted to grab him and hug him—but if she did, she probably wouldn't stop with just hugging. "Yes, it is."

"We've played a lot of phone tag so far, Sam and me. I never seem to get a moment to meet with them. He called again last Monday, as we were about to get in the car for the trip here. I felt guilty that I've kept putting him off, so I said if he and Mia were willing to come up to Valentine Bay, we could meet here, at the cottage. They're coming tomorrow afternoon. Between you and me, it's mostly a formality. I'm going to see that they get what they need from

Stryker Marine, but I like a nice face-to-face before I seal a deal."

"I would love to be an eavesdropper at that meeting."

"You want to hire someone to build you a container home?"

"I'm just interested. I minored in architecture at UO, and my senior project was hands-on with four classmates. We built a tiny container home right there on campus."

"Architecture? I thought you were all theater, all the time."

She realized she'd never explained her plans to him. "I'm thinking of changing things up career-wise, hoping maybe to get a paid intern job with an architectural firm—or an entry-level position in a company that designs the spaces people live in. I'm qualified right now to be a residential designer. And I'm planning on going back to school. I want a master's in architecture from a NAAB-accredited college. And you're helping me toward my new life goals, so thank you for that."

He looked confused, but interested, too. "Hey. Whatever I can do—which is what, exactly?"

"You pay me well and I'm socking every penny away to move to Seattle in February. U-Dub in Seattle offers an accredited master's degree. As for my next job, I've been applying for anything promising that comes up, but I think I'll have better luck if I'm already in town and don't have to relocate when the right job comes around."

"Whoa." He finished off his glass. "You're leaving Valentine Bay?"

"I am, yes."

"What about your sister, the director? You two are close, aren't you? And doesn't she count on you to run the technical side of things?"

"She does, yeah. But our lighting director can do my job. He'll step up to the tech director position when I go. As for Hailey and me, I'll miss her a lot. However, I just need to get out there and discover what I really want out of life. I love the theater. And yet I've always had this dream of helping to create the places people actually live and work. And Seattle's not *that* far away. I'll come home often."

He turned his body her way and brushed a hand against her shoulder. The simple touch shivered through her. "Why not try Portland? It's closer."

She loved that he would even suggest she might move to *his* town. But she shook her head. "Seattle's a bigger market. More opportunities."

"Yeah, but you know *me*, and I know a lot of people in Portland. Never hurts to use your connections. Networking is what it's all about."

He was right. Too bad she was so powerfully attracted to him. The attraction made using him to get her new start feel wrong, somehow. "I don't think so, Linc."

He held her gaze. Her lips kind of tingled with the memory of kissing him. She wanted to do that again.

But right now, kissing him again seemed as unwise as agreeing to move to Portland and using his connections to find a job.

She backed away a fraction.

He did the same. "If you change your mind, you only need to let me know."

"Thanks."

He picked up the half-empty bottle of champagne. She set her glass beside his and he refilled them both.

When he handed hers back, he said, "The Acevedos will be here at two tomorrow. You should meet them."

She started to turn down the offer, on principle.

But he did have a point. She'd pretty much decided to switch her career focus from theater to architecture. That meant she needed to make connections with people in the business of construction and design. Plus, container buildings fascinated her. "It's doable. I can take the kids to the theater at one. Hailey will make sure that Maya is taken care of…"

"It's settled then. Leave the kids at the theater for an hour or two and I can introduce you to Sam and Mia."

Sam Acevedo was a big guy with sandy hair and a ready smile. Harper liked him at lot.

She liked Mia even more.

A tiny woman with thick, wavy black hair and striking obsidian eyes, Mia was sharp and so creative. She loved that Harper had helped build a container home in college. The two of them talked design ideas. By the end of the meeting, they'd exchanged digits and promised to keep in touch.

In the meantime, Sam and Linc had made a deal. Acevedo Hybrid Homes would be acquiring shipping containers from Stryker Marine at a deeply discounted price.

When the couple drove off in their quad cab, Linc shut the door and turned to Harper. "Move to Portland. I'll bet you can get yourself a job with Mia and Sam."

She laughed. The guy was shameless, but in such an appealing way. "They're a start-up—you said it yourself. They've been in business for what—three years? They don't need a design intern at this point."

"They need to grow, and that means soon they'll have to hire someone to work with Mia on the design front. Why shouldn't that someone be you?"

She avoided answering that loaded question by observing, "Sometimes you remind me of Hailey."

He frowned. "That's good, right?"

"You're both so certain that you know what needs to happen next and how to make it happen."

"In this case, I do know what needs to happen— you, working with Mia and Sam."

"Yeah, but sometimes you have to let other people find their own way."

"Nah. I know better."

She gave him the side-eye. "What did I tell you? Just like my sister—and come to think of it, Roman's kind of that way, too. He and Hailey are always getting crossways with each other because *she* knows how it has to be, and so does *he*, and their ideas of how it has to be don't always match up."

Linc's frown had deepened. "But see, I know I'm right about this."

"Oh, of course you are. But I'm still doing it my way—and right now, I need to get back to the theater."

"Wait." He caught her arm.

Her stomach hollowed out, just from the warmth of his strong fingers pressing, imprinting themselves on her skin through the long-sleeved T-shirt she wore. "What?"

"I keep meaning to drop by over there, see what it's all about." His voice was low, half-teasing.

She answered in kind—softly. "Are you saying you want to come with?"

"Yeah." His eyes were on hers. She could stand here in the front hall forever, just the two of them, his warm hand still wrapped around her arm. "I think I will."

"That's good." She wanted to reach up, thread her fingers into the thick, coffee-brown hair at his temples, feel the texture of it against her fingertips. "I like Mia. A lot."

"I had a hunch you would."

"Thank you, for encouraging me to sit in on your meeting."

"You're welcome. Networking. It's what it's all about."

Reluctantly, she eased her arm free of his grip. "You coming or not?"

He grabbed the key from the bowl by the door. "Let's get out of here."

Linc was thoroughly enjoying himself. Things were good with him and Harper again, and he really liked just being with her.

It continually surprised him, how easy and right he felt around her. She kind of put a whole new light on everyday activities. Even a short drive to the old theater downtown became fun and interesting.

She pointed out the twisting driveway up to old Angus McTerly's house as they passed it. A few minutes later, when they entered the historic district, she showed him the art gallery that Daniel's wife, Keely, owned and ran.

He constantly found himself thinking that from now until New Year's wasn't going to be enough for him when it came to her. He needed more time to get to know everything about her, which was why he'd decided that he would keep after her until he convinced her that Portland was the place for her.

Lucky for him, he had five days a week for the next month—more if he could get her to work a few weekends, too. Surely in that amount of time he could make her see that she would find the right job for her in Rose City.

"Here we are," she said, and pointed at an empty parking space right there on the street twenty feet from the front entrance of the Valentine Bay Theatre. He pulled the SUV in at the curb.

The theater was one of those classic 1920s movie and vaudeville palaces. Outside, it had a lot of plaster moldings and Moorish-looking arches. Inside, it was white stucco walls, more arches and thick pillars holding up the lobby ceiling.

Harper led him into the auditorium where Hailey, with Maya on her hip, paced back and forth in front of the stage. Maya seemed content to chew on her blue teething toy and stare at Hailey with rapt fascination as Harper's sister directed a large group of kids through a song centered on a lost angel on Christmas morning—or something like that.

It was hard to tell what the song was about, exactly. The kids up on stage kept laughing and arguing as Hailey and a very calm, statuesque woman with dark copper skin and light brown hair coiled in thick locks tried to corral them and get them to focus.

"This is the finale," Harper whispered in his ear just as he spotted Jayden up there on the stage snickering at something the little girl standing next to him had said. "It's their first time through it."

No kidding, he thought.

The lights kept changing—flashing and blinking,

going very low and then suddenly flaring blindingly bright. Apparently, the guy up in the light booth was working something out in the middle of rehearsal.

The accompanist, on piano, patiently stopped and started as kids interrupted to ask questions, and Hailey called a halt every few minutes to give suggestions and then have them go over this or that section of the unrecognizable song yet again.

Beside him, Harper whispered, "What do you think?"

Looked like pure chaos to him. But he was having a good time watching the confusion unfold. The kids seemed happy and he was sitting next to Harper. He couldn't think of anywhere else he would rather be. "Great!" he replied with a lot more enthusiasm than the disaster up on the stage could possibly inspire.

Harper chuckled. The sound sent a ripple of pure pleasure rolling through him. How strange that just the sound of her laugh gratified him in a physical way. He thought of Alan Hollister, sitting in the kitchen at the West Hills house in Portland last Monday morning right before he and Jean left for the airport. The older man's face had lit up with pure happiness when he heard Jean laugh in delight at something Jayden had said.

Even when Linc was a boy and his parents were still making an effort to give him and Megan a real family life, he'd never seen his father react to his mother as if she captivated him completely the way Jean did Alan.

"I know what you see right now looks like a catastrophe in the making." Harper's warm breath teased his ear. "But wait till the opening performance. The children want to do their best and they will. It always turns out beautifully."

He gave up the pretense of admiring the so-called show and turned to gaze directly into those gorgeous gray-blue eyes. "If you say so…"

"Lincoln Stryker, when have I ever steered you wrong?"

He couldn't help slanting a quick glance at her supple mouth. That mouth had him remembering Thanksgiving night and the steaming-hot kisses they'd shared. He wanted to kiss her again. If he ever got that chance, he would have sense enough not to ruin a perfect moment with apologies.

Yeah, more than once over the weekend without her, he'd promised himself that if she would only come back to help him with the kids, he would keep it strictly business.

But that was then. Now, with her beside him, he knew he'd only been lying to himself. No way was he keeping his distance from Harper Bravo.

She was a revelation to him, so different from the women he'd been with before—sophisticated women, who harbored secret agendas, incurious women, completely uninterested in other people's children.

Yeah. A revelation. That was Harper Bravo.

And he wanted more of her. She'd already made

it excruciatingly clear that she didn't consider herself his employee, that she was a free agent and her own boss. Any intimacy they shared would be because they both wanted it. Didn't that clear the way for him to get to know her better?

Sure seemed like it to him.

From now on, he wouldn't miss any opportunity to get up close and personal with her.

Chapter Six

"So how about a movie or something?" he suggested that night when they met at the foot of the stairs after putting the kids to bed. His pulse thrummed in his ears as he waited for her answer. He just knew he would crash and burn. That she would look at him regretfully and say it wasn't a good idea.

But then she grinned. "Sure. First, though, I have to run over to my cottage and grab a few things I need to work on."

Yes! She said yes!

His pulse throbbed all the harder, with triumph. He could barely hear himself think and wondered vaguely if he might be a candidate for a sudden, early heart attack.

"What things?" he demanded. Not that it mattered in the least. She could bring a trailer full of woodworking equipment and set up shop in the living room, get a power saw going in there for all he cared.

She leaned a little closer. He caught a sweet whiff of vanilla and lemons and had to resist the urge to pull her into his arms. "Some of the costumes for the Christmas show need minor alterations and repairs," she explained. "I can do those while we watch."

"Fair enough. Popcorn?"

"Sounds pretty much perfect to me."

She left. By the time she came back ten minutes later, he had the popcorn ready. She took a Perrier and he had a beer. They sat on the sofa, with the tree blazing bright and the outdoor lights winking beyond the picture windows.

At her feet sat a basket full of stuff that needed mending.

He set the bowl of popcorn on the coffee table, plunked his ass nice and close to her and picked up the remote. "So, a romantic comedy?"

She slanted him a look. "I'm in the mood for horror. Something really gory would be fun."

He kind of got off on just looking at her. She seemed to glow from within and he loved her pointy little chin and prominent cheekbones. And those dimples...

He could write poetry about those dimples of hers.

Which was pretty damn spooky. Linc Stryker had never written a poem in his life.

She glanced up from mending a split seam on a set of plush antlers mounted on a fuzzy brown headband. "Not a fan of horror movies, huh?"

"Hmm?"

"Horror movies. You don't like them?"

He realized he'd been staring at her—ogling her, really—and felt more than a little embarrassed. "Oh. No—I mean, I've got no problem with horror movies. You just surprised me is all."

"Oh, right. Because I'm a woman, I should automatically want to watch a love story."

"Whoa. Did I say that? I don't remember saying that."

"Good—not that I don't love a good love story..."

"Uh. Great to know."

"It's just sometimes I want the blood and the gore."

"I understand." *Maybe. A little...*

She stuck her needle in the antler and neatly pulled the thread through. "All right, then. Let's have a look at our options."

He spoke into the remote and several choices came up on the big screen mounted above the fireplace.

She pointed at an image of a teenage blonde clutching a bloody knife standing in front of a Christmas tree. "That's the one. It's got Christmas and babysitting and home invasion, too."

He wanted to whip the plush antlers out of her hands and kiss that full mouth of hers. "You're a bloodthirsty thing, aren't you?"

And she laughed. "You'd better believe it." She instructed, "Keep the sound down low and turn on the subtitles."

"Why?"

"We don't want the kids waking up and hearing screams downstairs."

"Bloodthirsty, but thoughtful. It's an intriguing combination…"

"Give me that." She reached over and tried to whip the remote from his hand.

He yanked it away, up over his head, and faked a horrified expression. "What are you *doing*?"

She laughed again—a full-throated laugh this time. The sound echoed through him, leaving shimmers of happiness in its wake. "You're such a *man*," she accused. "Heaven forbid, you should lose control of the remote."

He lowered the device, pressed it close to his heart and solemnly intoned, "Never, ever try to come between a man and his remote."

She grabbed for it again. He let her get hold of it—that brought her in good and close. The scent of her taunted him.

And then he whipped the remote free of her grip, threw it over the back of the sofa and grabbed for her, smashing the plush antlers between their bodies, making her laugh all the harder.

She let out a yelp followed by more laughter and wriggled against him, trying to tickle him back as he tickled her.

Tickled her. When in his whole life had he ever tickled anyone—not including Megan, back when they were kids? When had he ever had fun with a woman, just being silly and playful, wrestling for the remote?

He realized at that moment that he'd never had a lot of silliness in his life and he needed more of it. More of *her*.

She squealed and shoved at him. He rolled, taking her with him. They fell to the rug between the sofa and coffee table, him on the bottom, her on top. She felt like heaven, so soft and curvy, round in all the right places, and she smelled so good. Her unbound hair fell all around them, a waterfall of wheat-colored silk.

A funny little sound escaped her—a hitch of breath on a tiny moan as she craned her upper body away to stare down at him through those enormous pale blue eyes. "We're crushing my antlers." She lifted up enough to pull the smashed headpiece from between their bodies. He stifled a groan as her movement rubbed him where it mattered.

"Here." He took the antlers from her. Reaching across her body, he slid them onto the coffee table next to the untouched bowl of popcorn.

"Thanks." She relaxed on top of him, lowering her head so their noses were only a few inches apart, bringing that mouth he couldn't wait to taste again so excitingly close. He was lost in those eyes of hers. They had a rim of darker blue around the iris. From inches away, he could see gold flecks fanning out from the midnight of her pupils.

She looked like an angel and she felt like everything he'd ever needed without even knowing it, all softness and the promise of some brighter, better future ahead, where there would be laughter and long talks about his day and her day—and in the morning, kids in the kitchen demanding blueberry pancakes.

He needed to kiss her. But first, he had to be sure that he wasn't overstepping or misreading the situation. He asked in a voice rough with desire, "Yes or no?"

The minute he asked the question, he felt ridiculous. *Yes or no?* The question made no sense—not even to him, and he was the one who had asked it.

But she understood. She understood exactly. Lifting a hand, she guided a heavy lock of hair behind her ear. It only fell down again and brushed against his cheek, smelling of lemons, satiny and warm. "I *want* to…"

She wants to! He resisted the urge to let out a shout of elation and instead asked quietly, "But?"

"Well, I mean, yes, if we're agreed it's just for now…nights, you know? When the kids are in bed?"

"A secret?" He didn't want to put boundaries on

anything he might share with her. But he didn't want to scare her off again, either.

"Not exactly. I mean, really, I don't care who knows. I like you. You like me. There's nothing to sneak around about—except for the kids. If they see us all over each other, they'll get ideas. They'll start to think we might end up together in a more permanent way, begin to expect that I will be around after New Year's."

So? he almost asked. After all, the way he saw it, keeping her around after New Year's was pretty much the goal.

And who was to say his niece and nephew didn't already think of Harper as part of their lives? Of course, they would miss her when he took them back home to Portland.

Unless she came with them.

She went on, "It would confuse them, Jayden especially. Maya's a little young to get what it might mean if she saw us kissing or whatever. But we would definitely have to be discreet around Jayden."

He stroked her velvety cheek and then guided that misbehaving lock of hair back over her shoulder. "I'll make that deal. For now. Subject to change, though, if we realize it could be more."

"But that's my point. It really can't be more."

"Wrong. You don't know what will—"

"Shh." She put two soft fingers against his mouth. He wanted to suck them inside, to scrape them with his teeth. "Now you're shushing me?" He said it gently, teasing her.

But she didn't smile. She gazed down at him, all seriousness. "You run your own company, Linc. You have two beautiful children to raise. Your life going forward is clear to you. *You* know who *you* are. I still have things to figure out. About myself. About my life. I'm not in a place to start building a lasting relationship. For me, right now, there really can't be *more*. It would have to end at New Year's when you and the kids go back to Portland."

He took her sweet face between his hands. "You don't know what will happen in a month. I'm just asking you not to close the door on the very real possibility that we both might want more."

She pushed away from him. He made himself let her go and stifled a pained groan when she rocked back off his groin. They both sat up and stared blankly at the big screen above the mantel. Finally, she said in a resigned little voice, "I'm still uncomfortable about your engagement."

Defensiveness tightened his gut. "What's to be uncomfortable about? I told you it's over. She broke it off and it was the right thing to do. It wasn't working, and we wouldn't have been happy together."

"But you were going to get *married*. When you love someone, you don't just stop. It's a…process, isn't it? It takes time to work through the loss and the unmet expectations and the changes in your life."

He pushed the coffee table away enough that he

could draw his legs up and wrap his arms loosely around his knees. The bald, ugly truth probably wouldn't help him much here. But it was all he had to give her. "I didn't love Imogen—her name is Imogen Whitman. I never loved her."

Harper's mouth formed a perfect O.

"Now I've shocked you."

She fiddled with her hair, rolling a curl around a finger, easing it back behind her ear. "Yeah. I mean, why would you ask someone to marry you if you didn't love them?"

"I was almost thirty." When she started to speak, he put up a hand. "Let me finish?"

She gave a slow nod. "Sorry. Of course."

He stared into the fire as he tried to figure out how to explain himself. "I was approaching the big three-O. I was doing well running Stryker Marine. I wasn't seeing anyone steadily, but I wanted to get married, to have a family. I saw it as the next step for me. Imogen and I had grown up together. We went to the same schools. Her mother and mine are life-long friends. Imogen and I knew the same people. I thought all that meant we had a lot in common, that we would make a good match. Eventually, I found out I was wrong."

Harper drew her own legs up and rested her cheek on her knees. Her gaze probed his. "What made you realize that?"

"Megan and Kevin died."

She seemed to be waiting for him to say more. When he didn't, she prompted, "Yeah, and...?"

He hung his head. "You really want the details?"

"What I want is to understand. And I don't. Not yet."

He tried again. "My sister and her husband died the week of my wedding."

"How awful."

"Yeah. It was a big deal, the wedding. Imogen had been planning it forever, a lavish destination event on St. Bart's, two hundred guests. We had to cancel."

She thought about that. "Well, really. What else could you do?"

He almost smiled. "See? You get it. Imogen didn't—I mean, yes, she knew there was no getting around it, with my sister dying the same week as our big day. But we could've just gotten married quietly."

"But you didn't want that?"

"At that point I did, yes. I suggested it, as a matter of fact. It wasn't what she wanted. She wanted a killer wedding."

"That's not unusual, Linc. Most women do."

He had to ask. "Do *you* want a killer wedding?"

"I don't really think about my wedding yet. Right now, I'm all about finding the right job, getting my life on track."

"You're just trying to be fair to my ex."

"I suppose I am. I can see how it would have been hard for her. She had you all to herself and then suddenly, her beautiful wedding was on hold and you had two children to bring up."

"True. And she was bitter about it. She didn't like that I moved Kevin's parents into my house, either. The kids, taking custody of them, having them in my life—they changed everything. For me. Not for Imogen. She felt cheated. She said so, and she kept after me to reschedule the wedding. I put her off. Then, she decided we needed a romantic getaway, over Christmas, just her and me. I told her I couldn't do that. I needed to bring the kids here, to the cottage, give them what I could of the Christmas they would have had if we hadn't lost Megan and Kevin. And I needed to send Jean and Alan on the cruise of their dreams as a thank-you for everything they'd done."

She was watching him so closely. "I'm guessing from your expression that your fiancée wasn't going for it?"

"You guessed right. Imogen hit the roof and delivered an ultimatum. I was to forget sending the grandparents on a cruise—Jean and Alan could easily do that sometime after New Year's, she said. For Christmas, the grandparents would stay home with the kids. I would go away with *her* for the holidays, just the two of us. If I said no to her plans, she and I were through."

"And you said no."

"Yes, I did. She broke our engagement. End of story." He should probably tell her about Imogen's call last week.

Then again, no. Really. He was done with Imogen. And hadn't he said enough about the whole depressing situation already?

Her expression thoughtful, Harper regarded him steadily. "You were relieved when she broke it off with you?"

"I was, yeah."

"You really *didn't* love her, did you?"

He felt like crap at the moment. "I just told you I didn't." He sounded pissed off to his own ears.

And maybe he was, a little.

She said, "I'm not getting on your case—I'm really not. I can see your position. But, well, I do sympathize with her."

"Terrific," he grumbled.

"You're defensive about this."

He bit back a harsh response. Because she was right. "Yeah, maybe. A little. Or a lot…"

"What I'm trying to say is, if you *had* loved her, I think you would have been more understanding of how she felt. You would have realized that you needed to put her first at least some of the time, to reassure her that she was a high priority for you."

It really annoyed him how right she was. What else could he do but admit it? "You do have a point. I should have been more understanding. I thought I was happy with her. I really did. It's embarrassing to me now, but I honestly didn't know any better. Until my sister died and left the kids with me, until Jean and Alan moved in to help me out and I saw what a happy marriage was—up till then, I had no idea of the path I was on."

"What path was that?" Her voice was gentle, her eyes warm. She really didn't seem to be passing judgment on him. And yet he felt like he was messing everything up, telling her all this.

He admitted, "I was on the road to being just like my father. A first wife who was everything everyone I knew expected me to marry. And then a trophy wife. And then a third wife half my age."

A wistful smile curved her lips. "I've been wondering about your parents."

"That they're nowhere in sight, you mean, at Christmas, when their grandchildren have been orphaned and families are supposed to be together?"

"No, more that I pictured them as loving and supportive. Apparently, I got that wrong?"

"Well, they tried, when Megan and I were kids. But they were never what you would call happy together. They were two people from 'good' families who did what was expected of them—until my dad decided life was passing him by and the way to fix that was to trade my mom in on a younger model."

"So…" She let the word trail off, her gaze locked on his.

Had he blown it completely? Was she about to leap up and run out the door again? "What?"

"We're both at a place of change in our lives. You aren't getting married, after all, and you've got two kids to take care of for the next twenty years or so.

As for me, I'm trying to figure out the whole career thing."

He wanted to touch her, to trail his fingers over her cheek, smooth her hair. Anything to make contact. To reassure himself and her that everything was right between them.

Because as soon as he'd started in about Imogen, everything started to feel all wrong.

He kept his hands to himself.

"Back to my original question..." She frowned.

He teased, "After that grim trip down memory lane, who can remember the original question?"

She giggled, and the knot of tension in his belly eased. "About you and me, till New Year's?"

"Right. I remember now. And I want that, Harper. I want to be with you till New Year's. Do you want to be with me?"

She faced him directly. "I do. Yes."

His heart bounced around in his chest again, doing fist pumps and cartwheels. "Whew. I really thought I'd blown it."

She bit her lip again and slowly shook her head. "I think you were honest. I appreciate that."

He did dare then, to reach out and touch her. Slowly, he traced a finger along the fine, pure line of her jaw. "And will you keep an open mind about the two of us, about what will happen after the holidays...?"

"Hmm." She chewed on her bottom lip.

He wrapped his arm around her and pulled her

close to him. She went willingly, even leaning her head on his shoulder with the sweetest little sigh. He pressed a kiss to the tender flesh at her temple. "Well?"

She snuggled even closer. "Okay. I will. I'll keep an open mind about the future." She looked up at him then. Her big eyes were so serious, so very determined. "As long as you know where I stand. I need to go to Seattle. First and foremost, I need to make my own life and feel good about it. If we take this any further, it should be just for fun, with the understanding that it ends when you return to Portland."

"An understanding that we can revisit before we say goodbye."

She gave a quick dip of her pretty chin. "Yes."

He knew he couldn't push for more. She wouldn't go there. But at least, she'd promised to reconsider a possible next step for them when the holidays were over. "All right."

She tucked her head under his chin, and he tightened his arm around her. "Now what?" she asked.

Easing his fingers beneath the fall of her hair, he cradled the back of her neck and waited for her to look up at him again.

When she did, he lowered his mouth to hers.

She accepted his kiss with an urgent little sound. He drank that sound into him and deepened the contact as she raised her arms and wrapped them around his neck.

Still kissing her, savoring the taste of her, he pushed the coffee table away enough to turn fully toward her and rise to his knees. She stretched her body up to him, chasing the kiss, her thick yellow hair tumbling down her back. He caught her face between his hands and then raked his fingers backward into the warm, satiny strands.

She let out a sweet, hot growl from low in her throat. He drank it down.

Satisfied that she seemed to want him as much as he wanted her, he guided her to her back again. It wasn't really a comfortable spot, between the table and the sofa. And now that he was on top, he worried that he might be crushing her.

But she was beautifully willing, wrapping her soft arms around his neck as her tongue played with his, bringing a rough, needful groan from him, one that echoed inside his head.

Had he ever felt like this? Full of urgency and longing, overexcited, burning for more?

As a kid, maybe? His first time?

Yeah—but then again, no.

There'd been nothing like this in his life, nothing like Harper, in his arms, saying yes to him with every hitch of breath, every tender sigh, every slide of her naughty tongue against his...

Her clever hands drifted down to press against his chest. She grabbed his shirt in her fists and yanked him even closer.

Closer was good. Closer was excellent. He was

achingly hard now, his straining fly pressed to the cove of her sex. Even with all the layers of their clothing between them, he could feel the welcoming heat of her, revel in the way she rocked her hips into him. She was so open to him, hungry for everything, her mouth and her clutching hands demanding all he could give her, eager to give in return.

He could not wait.

Time to get her upstairs, lock the door, become intimately familiar with every inch of her underneath her clothes…

But then, with a desperate moan, she flattened her hands at his chest again. Instead of pulling him closer, she pushed.

Oh, hell no.

She wouldn't.

She *couldn't*…

But apparently, she could and she would.

Carefully lifting away from her, he sucked in a slow breath and ordered his raging hard-on to chill.

She gazed up at him, flushed and so pretty, her hair a tangled halo around her angel's face. He gritted his teeth and waited for her to say they had to stop.

Almost shyly, she caught her tongue between her teeth. He would have sacrificed last quarter's profits at Stryker Marine to be the one biting that tongue of hers.

"I think," she said with a tender little smile, "we probably ought to take this upstairs."

Damn. She wasn't calling a halt, after all. He blinked in elated disbelief. "Yeah?"

Her smile trembled wider. "Yes, please."

"Excellent idea." With care, he eased one knee to the rug between her legs and the other on the outside of her left thigh. "Let me help you." He offered his hand and she took it. Rising, he pulled her up with him. "This way." Still holding her hand, he turned for the stairs.

She hung back. "We never ate our popcorn..."

He snatched up the bowl. "We'll take it with us, in case you want some later."

She laughed. "Where's the remote? We should turn off the TV." Over the mantel, the screen saver had activated. An ad for a streaming service bounced around in the blackness.

"I think I threw it behind the sofa." He tugged on her hand again, but she stayed where she was. Impatient, he faced her again. "Say it."

She only looked at him. God, she was so beautiful. Kind of...pure and somehow untouched. An angel in old jeans and a baggy sweater, with messy hair.

"Fine," he grumbled. "Hold the damn popcorn."

She took the bowl from his hand.

He circled the sofa, grabbed the remote and pointed it at the TV. The screen went completely dark. "Happy now?"

"Thank you." She stepped to the end of the sofa and then rounded it toward him.

He tossed the remote on the sofa cushions and reached for her, getting her by her free hand and guiding it around behind him so he could slide one arm under her knees and the other at her back.

She let out a silly squeal as he lifted her high against his chest. Popcorn went flying.

"Don't you even expect me to stop and pick those up," he grumbled.

She held the popcorn bowl in her lap now and reached out her free hand to touch his face. "Okay," she whispered, her eyes locked with his.

He kissed her, standing there behind the sofa, loving the feel of her, right here, in his arms.

When he let her mouth go, she taunted, "The fire's still on."

There was a remote for it, too. But there was also a switch next to the mantel. He carried her over there and she turned it off.

That left the lamps at either end of the sofa—and the tree and the outside lights. He shook his head before she could go there. "The lamps can stay on. The tree and the outdoor lights are on timers. They'll turn off at midnight."

"The baby monitor?" she asked. It sat on a side table by the wing chair a few feet from the sofa.

"Leave it. There's another one up in my room."

She kissed him again. "All right. Let's go upstairs."

In the master bedroom, he set her down on the thick gray rug by the bed, took the popcorn from her and carried it to a table in the sitting area. He locked the door to the hallway.

When he returned to her, she lifted her arms and twined them around his neck. He needed to kiss her, so he did, taking her mouth gently, teasing her lips to open as she started unbuttoning his shirt.

"Clothes. Who needs them?" He kissed the words across her left cheek and then bit the tip of her chin— gently, of course.

She made a soft sound of agreement. And then she stepped back. He was about to beg her to touch him again when she grabbed the hem of her big sweater and whipped it off over her head. Ripping the zipper of her jeans wide, she shoved them down.

Captivated, he watched as she kicked off the short boots she wore and tore off her socks. When she stood before him, delectable in a yellow satin bra and little white panties, she demanded, "Why are you still fully dressed?"

He looked her up and down. Slowly. "It's too much fun just looking at you. I want to kiss every inch of you."

She tipped her head sideways with a thoughtful frown. "Hmm. I do like the way you say that."

But when he reached for her, she jumped back, shaking her head. "Come on, Linc. Everything off."

No problem. He went to work on the buttons of his shirt, picking up where she left off. When that took too long, he grabbed hold of it in either hand and pulled. She laughed as those last buttons went flying. He yanked on one sleeve and then the other and tossed the shirt away.

Her smile bloomed wide. "Now you're talkin'." She watched, nodding in approval, as he stripped off everything else. "Oh, my," she said on a sweet, breathy sigh when he stood in front of her naked. "Lincoln Stryker, you look even better minus your clothes." She stepped in close and put those nimble hands of hers on his chest, whispering, "I really like all these muscles." Her fingers strayed, wandering down over his belly, back up and outward to caress his shoulders. Shivers trickled down his spine with every touch. "My, my, my," she added softly when she tipped her head down and saw how glad he was to be here with her. But then she glanced up with a look of alarm. "Tell me you have condoms. I get the shot, but…"

"Don't explain. I do know the rules." It was their first time together, and even if he felt like he'd been waiting his whole life for her show up, they had only just met a week ago yesterday. They had a mutual obligation to be safe in every sense. Yanking open the bedside drawer, he grabbed a few Magnums and dropped them within easy reach. "Come here." He pulled her nice and tight against him. Claiming her mouth again, he unhooked her pretty bra.

She yanked it out from between their bodies, and he felt her naked breasts, soft and full, pressing into his chest, her nipples like pebbles, so hard and tight.

Was this really happening—him and Harper? At last…

So what if he'd known her for only a week and a day? It seemed he'd waited forever to be with her like this. He'd been hoping for this moment, longing for it, even going so far as to overnight the condoms from Amazon just in case.

Now that he had her in his arms, all he really wanted was never to have to let her go. She tasted so good and she felt exactly right, as though every smooth, soft inch of her had been fashioned just for him.

Scooping her high again, he set her on the bed. She pulled him down on top of her, hooking one silky, bare leg over his hip, sucking his tongue into her mouth.

He rolled them so they lay facing each other. That way he could touch her more easily. Palming the inward curve of her waist, he slid his hand upward to cup one fine, plump breast.

She moaned and then whimpered into his mouth as he flicked the tight nipple with his thumb. Nothing compared to her, to the sounds of desire she made, to the giving feel of her flesh under his hand.

He needed to touch all of her, to kiss every secret hollow and gorgeous curve. With some reluctance, he took his mouth from hers, but only to kiss his way down the side of her throat, nipping and licking as he went. The scent of her swam around him, sweet and tart and perfect, as he nuzzled the tight skin over the delicate ridge of her collarbone.

It wasn't far from there, just a scattering of quick

kisses downward, and he was sucking a nipple into his mouth.

She called out his name then, her fingers fisting in his hair as she lifted her body to him, offering him more.

He took it, sucking hard, swirling his eager tongue around the pebbled tip, letting his hand stray downward over the silky curve of her belly and under the waistband of those innocent white panties.

Another cry escaped her as his fingers found her. She was wet and so willing, raising her hips to him, offering him everything he couldn't wait to claim.

"Oh, Linc…" she whispered.

"Off," he commanded, hooking his thumbs in at the side of the panties, shoving them down.

She wiggled, chuckling a little, as he worked at pushing the panties below her knees and she kicked them off the rest of the way. He watched them drop off the tip of her toe, over the side of the bed.

"So pretty…" He admired the golden, neatly trimmed hair at the top of her mound, petting her and then dipping his fingers into the womanly heart of her again.

He needed to be closer. He needed to taste her.

So he kissed his way down her body, lifted one smooth thigh over his shoulder and settled between her spread legs. Now he had full access to all her secrets.

She clutched his head between her hands and

surged up, opening her legs even wider, letting him kiss her long and slow and thoroughly.

When she came, she cried out again. He stayed with her, stroking her with his fingers, feeling the flutter of her climax against his tongue.

The moment the tiny pulses stopped, she was grabbing his shoulders, pulling him up to her, until they were eye to eye again. She seemed dazed, almost delirious.

He completely understood. He felt wild, free—different. Looking into the silver-blue heat of her eyes, he thought, *This. Right here. This woman. This moment.*

This was how it should be, just the two of them. Every night, for all the nights.

But he was still connected enough to reality *not* to say that to her right now.

Right now, he kissed her.

For a long time, and deeply.

She reached down between their bodies and wrapped her cool, slim hand around him. He groaned into her mouth as she stroked him, driving him close to the brink way too quickly.

In the end, he had to pull his mouth from hers and groan, "Harper. Inside you..."

Those lush, swollen lips bloomed into a wide, happy smile. "Yes, please."

So he flung out an arm to the nightstand and groped around until he found one of the condoms he'd dropped there. He had it out of the wrapper and rolled down over his aching length in seconds flat.

"Come here," she ordered. "Now…"

He couldn't obey fast enough.

She pulled him to her, wrapping an arm around his neck, opening her legs for him. He settled carefully on top of her and she reached down between them to take him in hand and guide him home.

Heaven, easing into her, feeling her body give to him as she opened slowly around him. She was so hot and tight. He gritted his teeth and thought of logistics, back-haul rates and suboptimization—exerting superhuman effort to put his mind on anything and everything but how good she felt and how close he was to going off like a bottle rocket when he'd yet to fully fill her.

"Linc," she whispered, pulling him closer, her sweet breath warm across his cheek.

And then her lips were there, meeting his. He kissed her, tasting her deeply. Fisting his hands in the glorious mess of her lemon-scented hair, he deepened the contact by aching degrees.

And by some miracle, he lasted. She was all around him now, silky arms and strong, long legs holding him to her, pulling him closer.

And closer still.

Until she owned him.

Only then, at last, did he allow himself to move. Withdrawing slowly at first and then sinking carefully back into her, he drank her pleasured cries. She lifted eagerly to meet his every thrust.

A revelation, to be with her like this. To be happy and perfectly content in the center of this private storm that raged between them. He'd never known anything so tender, so sweet and somehow, at the same time, so wild and free.

What was it about her?

She could speak to him without using any words. Her pretty face and soft, curvy body excited him, but even more, he took a deep pleasure in her giving spirit, her wicked sense of humor and the way she called him on his crap.

He had it all when she was wrapped around him, holding him tight. With her, he knew that anything was possible as long as he held her close to his heart.

It was the best kind of torture, the kind a man never wants to end, even as he chases his completion, needing the sweet release at the finish, but craving *her* satisfaction even more.

She gave it to him, rocking up into him, scratching his back with her short nails, groaning, "Yes," and "Right there," and "Oh, yes, Linc!" as she came again.

By then, he couldn't hold on for one second longer.

Growling low in his throat, he buried his face against the fragrant, sweat-damp crook of her neck. Heat shot up his spine, arrowed back down and finally exploded in the hot pulse of release.

Chapter Seven

They never did eat the popcorn.

Not that Harper really minded.

Instead, Linc led her into the bathroom and filled up the gorgeous slipper tub. He climbed in first, settling against the high back of the tub as she used a brush she found in the cabinet drawer under one of the sinks to work the worst tangles out of her hair and twist it up into a knot on top of her head.

"Come here," he said and held out a hand. She took it and got in. The water felt wonderful, hot and soothing, as he guided her to sit in front of him, between his powerful thighs, with his broad chest to rest against.

"Feels so good." She closed her eyes and just

drifted for a little while, managing somehow not to think too hard about the wisdom of what had just happened between them. Instead, she indulged in the sheer pleasure of this beautiful man cradling her, with his big arms around her, his fingers idly stroking up and down her arm.

Her body felt all warm and limp and well used. Being with Linc this way was something of a revelation to her. She'd always enjoyed sex, but tonight was the first time she'd been swept away by it. She was used to seeing the compelling connection between her happily coupled-up siblings. Not so much for herself, though.

But she saw it now, felt it right down to the core of her. Finally, with Linc, she got what all the shouting was about. It was amazing, like an electrical current sizzling between them. She intended to fully enjoy herself, take a walk on the sexy side, until the first of the year.

Linc's stroking fingers grew bolder. They slipped under the water.

The excitement between them bloomed to life all over again. Those big, long fingers brought her to another searing orgasm.

When she finished begging him never to stop, she rolled over and kissed his impressive erection, which bobbed above the water. And she didn't stop with just kissing.

He raised his hard hips up to meet her, rocking his body up and down as she took him into her eager mouth and let him slide out again, the water shifting and sloshing around them. It was glorious. He groaned her name as he came.

A little later, he helped her out of the deep tub and dried her off with a huge, fluffy white towel, taking his time about it, pausing now and then so they could indulge in slow, sweet kisses.

Eventually, they returned to the bedroom.

They started kissing again and things got intense. She was going to be sore tomorrow, but she only smiled to herself at the thought of that.

Harper Bravo, insatiable temptress. It had a nice ring to it, she thought.

It was after eleven when she reminded herself that she really ought to put on her clothes and go home. But she felt so contented and lazy. And here, under the covers with Linc in his big bed, it was cozy and warm. With a happy sigh, she snuggled in nice and close…

Maya's voice jolted her awake. "Unc Wink, up!"

There was a tap on the bedroom door, and Jayden called, "Uncle Linc, can I please come in?"

Morning light filtered through the shut blinds. From the other pillow, Linc watched her, his thick brown hair a tangled thatch. "Morning, beautiful."

Jayden tapped on the door again. "Maya wants up!"

"Unc Wink, I so hungwy!" insisted the little girl

from the monitor on Linc's nightstand, next to the discarded condom wrappers.

Harper groaned. "Busted."

Linc eased a warm hand around her nape, pulled her close for a quick kiss and then rolled away and stood. Grabbing his pants, he shoved his bare feet in them. Swiftly, he zipped up. Padding over to a bureau, he got a long-sleeved T-shirt. Pulling it on over his head, he returned to the bed.

"I'll wrangle the kids." He kept his voice to a whisper, so Jayden wouldn't hear them. "Give me fifteen minutes and then come on down to the kitchen. We'll let 'em think you just came over from your place."

She sat up and forked her messy hair back off her forehead. "I can't stick around," she whispered back. "Not if we're still going to Portland tomorrow?"

"Please, yes. I've got two days of damn meetings and I really need you there."

"Then I have to meet Hailey and Doug for break-fast in an hour. Doug requires a rundown of his tech director responsibilities while I'm away."

Linc frowned. "I just realized that Jayden and Maya will have to miss two days of rehearsal."

"Not a problem. I've already worked it out with Hailey. She'll catch them up when we get back. It's all going to be fine." Jayden knocked again. Maya had stopped using her words and started to fuss.

"Kids," he muttered. "You can never just ignore them."

She couldn't help laughing—but softly, so Jayden wouldn't hear. "Better get moving," she warned. "Before those two stage an insurrection. I'm just going to sneak out once you're downstairs."

He leaned across the bed and planted a kiss between her eyes. "I'll miss you."

"Not for long. I'll see you at one—now go." She gave him a playful shove.

After sticking his feet in a pair of mocs, he headed for the door, opening it just wide enough to slip through.

She grinned as she heard Jayden complain, "I thought you were *never* going to get up…"

That night, after Jayden and Maya were in bed, Harper happily followed Linc up to his room.

This time, she took her phone up with her and put it beside the bed, next to the handful of condoms he pulled from the drawer.

Her phone alarm went off at ten.

Linc tried to get her to stay. "Just for another hour. Eleven's not all that late…"

Was she tempted?

Yes, she was. She couldn't get enough of his kisses, of his perfect, tender touch. "I'll be back at seven in the morning, me and my suitcase, all ready to go…"

He caught her hand and pulled her against him on the bed in the tangle of covers from two bouts of enthusiastic lovemaking. "It's just an hour."

She laughed and kissed him. When he relaxed his hold, she rolled out of his reach and off the far side of the bed. Landing with her feet on the rug, she grabbed for her scattered clothes.

He appeared to accept the inevitable. Bracing his head on his hand, he watched her get dressed. "I don't like it when you leave."

She bent down to him again, but only long enough to grant him a quick kiss. "You looked so much like Jayden just then—you know, when he's sulking." Linc stuck out his bottom lip, clearly playing along. She chuckled. "Yup. Like uncle, like nephew."

He seemed resigned to her leaving by then. Still, he pretended to grab for her as she backed away. "Get back here."

"No can do." She dropped to a chair to tug on her socks and her short boots. "Tomorrow. Seven o'clock." She blew him a kiss as she slipped out the bedroom door.

Linc's stunning modern house in the West Hills sat within Forest Park on ten acres of manicured grounds with the urban forest all around.

They drove up the wide, curving driveway, through the futuristic silver gates to the soaring stone, glass and aluminum facade.

It was 9:45 a.m. Linc had his first meeting at the Stryker Marine complex at eleven.

Promising to return by six that night, he dropped them off with the luggage, leaving them in the care of the very capable and friendly housekeeper, Oxana, and a burly guy named Gus who took charge of the bags.

The housekeeper led Harper and her charges straight to the ultramodern kitchen, where the friendly cook, Wendy, greeted both children with hugs and a promise of a snack. She shooed Harper off with Oxana for a quick tour of the house and grounds.

The house offered breathtaking mountain views from every room on all three levels, a true marvel, with a soaring, two-story open living/dining room, an elevator and a soundproof media room, a home gym and an indoor pool in the walk-out basement.

Outside, a gorgeous series of interconnecting slate patios gave way to a smooth, limitless expanse of grass. Dark, lush forest loomed all around, with the panorama of the city below and snow-covered Mount Hood looming proudly in the distance.

Harper admired the sheer elegance and grace of it.

Was she a little intimidated? Maybe—and that wasn't a bad thing. So far, she loved being with Linc and she fully intended to savor each moment she had with him. It didn't hurt, though, to be reminded that his everyday life was nothing like hers and this magical Christmastime they'd decided to share was only for right now.

The kids had rooms on the top floor, to either side of the room Oxana had given Harper. The master suite, Linc's home office and another large bedroom were on the second floor flanking the enormous kitchen and living area. Hailey took time to unpack her suitcase and stick her things in the drawers in her room, though she doubted she would be sleeping there.

Down in the kitchen, the kids had finished their snacks. Harper took them to the playroom off the gym on the bottom floor.

"I swim!" announced Maya at the sight of the pool.

Jayden agreed that a swim was a great idea.

"We forgot to bring our suits," Harper reminded him.

"There are lots of suits in the playroom." Jayden took her hand and led her to a cabinet full of swimsuits in various sizes. She found suits for Maya and Jayden and one for herself, too.

Maya's was a pullup seahorse-themed swimsuit diaper. Jayden chose a pair of trunks printed with dinosaurs. Harper shut the three of them in the playroom and asked Jayden to look after Maya so she could slip into the small bathroom there and put on the white tank suit she'd found in her size. She knotted her long hair up into a bun at the top of her head and rejoined the children.

"There's water toys in here." Jayden pulled open another tall cabinet. Harper found a Maya-sized life jacket with floaties attached and a swim tube and goggles for Jayden.

The kids loved it. They splashed around in the

shallow end. Harper hung out with them, guiding them back to their end whenever they strayed too close to deep water.

Maya spent most of their swim slapping her floaties, seeing how big a splash she could make. Jayden was more adventurous. He put on his goggles and dipped his head under the water, after which he puttered around in his swim tube. At one point, he even managed to steamboat from one side of the shallow end to the other.

An hour into the fun, both kids grew tired. Jayden sat on the pool steps and tried to convince Harper that, as long as they were here in the Portland house, they really ought to decorate the place for Christmas.

"Don't you think the house might be a little bit sad, Harper, not to get any Christmas decorations at all because we're not here to make it *festive* and pretty?"

"I pwetty!" cried Maya, and slapped at the water. She laughed as water flew in all directions.

"Yes, you are so pretty!" Harper enthusiastically agreed.

"Hawp, get me!" Maya launched herself toward Harper, who caught her, lifted her and swung her around as the little girl squealed in delight.

Harper complimented Jayden, "Good use of *festive.*"

Jayden pinched up his little mouth. "But, Harper, can we *decorate*?"

"We're only here until Saturday morning, so my guess is no."

Jayden let his head fall back and groaned at the gleaming white quartz ceiling. "But, Harp-errr..."

She blew a raspberry against Maya's neck. Maya chortled at the way it tickled as Harper suggested to Jayden, "But tomorrow evening, we might talk your uncle into a visit with Santa and a drive across the river to see the Christmas lights on Peacock Lane." On the east side of the Willamette River, Peacock Lane was famous for its holiday displays.

Jayden considered her alternative suggestions and reluctantly decided they would have to do. "Well, if we can't decorate, seeing Santa and some Christmas lights would be really good."

Through the glass wall that partitioned off the pool area, Harper watched the elevator doors slide open. A man got off. He was dressed in gray wool slacks and a gorgeous white cashmere sweater. His shoes looked like the kind made in Italy by an artisan cobbler. He was middle-aged, but very well-preserved—handsome, really. He caught sight of her in the pool and smiled in greeting.

It was Linc's smile—just a little bit more reserved.

When he came through the glass door to the pool area, Jayden spotted him. "Grandpa Warren?" he asked almost hesitantly.

The man was Linc's dad, then. And judging by

Jayden's tone, the boy didn't know this grandfather as well as he knew Alan Hollister.

"Hello, Jayden. How are you?" Warren Stryker gave the little boy a crisp nod, one that managed to telegraph zero eagerness to have a wet child coming at him for a hug.

Jayden stayed where he was. "Hello, Grandpa," he replied, achingly polite. "I am fine. It's nice to see you."

Maya said nothing. She clutched Harper a little tighter around the neck and stared at the tall, good-looking older man.

"You must be Harper Bravo," Warren said. "Oxana explained that you'll be looking after the children while Lincoln has them at the cottage in Valentine Bay. I'm Warren Stryker, Lincoln's father."

"Yes, I'm Harper." She gave Linc's dad a polite smile. "Great to meet you. Did Oxana explain that Linc is at the office until six?"

"She did, yes. I was aware that Linc was coming back to town for meetings today. I thought I would stop by, see if I could catch him before he went to the complex."

"Sorry, he's already gone."

"Yes, I realize that." Warren stuck his hands in his pockets. The face of his designer watch caught the light, winking at her. She recognized the brand. Great-uncle Percy had one of those, an old one passed down from his father, Captain Xavier Valentine. The cost of it would have paid for her move to Seattle and covered all her expenses for the next year—with money to spare in case of emergencies. A secret smile curved the lips that were too much like Linc's. "I believe I knew your mother, actually. Marie Valentine?"

"Valentine was her maiden name, yes."

"You look like her—and I know it was a long time ago, but I did hear that she and your father died in Thailand. I'm so sorry for that—we met at Stanford, Marie and I. That was before she married your father, of course, and before Lincoln's mother and I began dating."

"Ah." Harper pasted on a smile and wondered why she felt so uncomfortable. Maybe it was that Linc's dad seemed to be…assessing her, somehow. Measuring her against some unknown standard. At least he didn't seem disapproving in his assessment. That was good. Right?

Honestly, she had no idea what was going on here. Maya had buried her head against Harper's neck and Jayden came off the pool steps and back in the water. He hovered close to Harper's side.

Warren said, "Well. I'll try Lincoln again after six."

Harper nodded. "Great to meet you." Okay, she sounded way too sweet and weirdly insincere. But Warren Stryker seemed to have a definite agenda, and she had no idea what that might be.

He was at the glass door that led out to the eleva-tor before she realized she should have offered condolences on the loss of his only daughter. "Warren." He stopped and turned back. "I just wanted to say how much I liked and admired your daughter. I met Megan and Kevin last Christmas when they brought the kids to Valentine Bay. I'm so sorry for your loss."

His dark gaze slid away. "Yes, thank you. Megan was a ray of sunshine, always." With a final nod, he turned again and went through the door.

Linc texted at five thirty.

Sorry. This last meeting is running late. I should be there by seven.

By then, the staff had left. It was just Harper and the kids. She texted back:

No problem. I'll go ahead and feed Jayden and Maya.

Good idea. See you at seven.

She almost added that she missed him. But she caught herself. It would only sound clingy and what they had was a temporary thing. Plus, he was busy in his meeting and didn't need the distraction of unnecessary texts.

Right then, another text popped up. Miss you.

Grinning ear to ear, she texted back, Miss you, too.

* * *

When Linc finally got back to the house at quarter past seven, he was greeted by the welcome sight of Harper and the kids upstairs in the ensuite bathroom off Maya's room.

Jayden was already in his pajamas, but he enjoyed sitting by the tub and splashing with Maya, who was covered in bubbles and surrounded by floating rubber toys.

The kids greeted Linc gleefully and splashed with enthusiasm.

Harper, on a stool far enough back from the action that she wasn't soaked yet, gave him a big smile that made him feel rejuvenated after a long day of tiring encounters with colleagues and customers who expected him to have the answer to any and all of their questions and a satisfying solution to every problem.

"We went swimming, Uncle Linc," Jayden informed him. "Now we're washing the colleen off Maya."

Harper picked up a rubber bluebird that Maya had sent soaring and gently corrected, "Chlorine." She handed the toy to the toddler.

And Jayden nodded. "*Clore*-een."

"Perfect." She beamed at him and then asked Linc, "Hungry? Wendy did prime rib with these fluffy potatoes and glazed carrots. I had a foodgasm over it, I am not kidding you."

"What's a foodgasm?" Jayden demanded.

Harper answered sweetly, "It's when you really like your dinner."

"I had a foodgasm, too," said Jayden as he launched a rubber boat across the tub. "'Cept for the carrots. I don't really like cooked carrots."

Linc was careful to quell his grin. "Thanks, but we had something brought in when that last meeting went long." He and Harper shared a long look and all he could think of was later, the two of them, alone in his bed.

The com system chimed.

Harper asked, "A visitor?"

"Yeah. Someone at the front gate. I'll get it."

Out in the hallway, at one of the control panels, he engaged the *talk* function. "Yes?"

His father answered, "Hello, son. Just thought I would stop by, see how you're doing."

Warren Stryker rarely *just stopped by*. When he showed up, he always had an objective.

"Come on in." Linc punched the key that opened the gate and the one that unlocked the front door. "I'll be right down." Before he went, he stopped in the bathroom doorway to update Harper. "My father's here. Think you can handle the stories and the tucking in?"

"Of course—he dropped by this morning looking for you."

"Did he say what he wanted?"

She gave him a shrug. "Sorry, no."

He tapped his knuckles on the door frame. "I'll try to make it quick."

"No hurry."

He waved at the kids. "'Night, Jayden. Kisses, Maya."

Maya blew one of her lip-smacking kisses and Jayden sang out, "Good night, Uncle Linc!"

The sounds of their happy laughter followed him down the stairs.

His father had just come in the door. "Lincoln. Merry Christmas."

"Good to see you, Dad." Linc took his father's coat and hung it in the entry closet. "How about a drink?"

"Now you're talking."

They went to Linc's home office. He gestured at the teal blue tuxedo sofa and mid-century modern chairs over by the wall of windows. The view was of the city lights spread out below Forest Park and the broad shadow of Mount Hood looming off to the east in the night sky. His father took a seat on the sofa.

"What'll you have?" Linc asked.

"Brandy?"

"Works for me." He got out the snifters and poured the Courvoisier, passing one to his father and then taking a chair across the coffee table from him. "I thought you and Shelby were at home in Vail."

His father swirled the amber liquid in his glass. "Shelby's still there. I'll fly back tomorrow."

Linc had spent all day at the office and he didn't

want to dance around. He wanted to cuddle a little with his niece and nephew and then take Harper to bed. "What's going on, Dad?"

Warren pondered his drink. "Your mother called me from Italy."

Linc had a bad feeling. In the decade since Warren cheated on her and then dumped her for his secretary, Linc's mother had made it a point of pride not to give her ex-husband the time of day. At Megan's funeral, Alicia had snubbed him outright.

"I'm listening," Linc said.

"Your mother got a call from Sarah Whitman." Linc wasn't really surprised. After all, Imogen's mother and Alicia Buckley Stryker had been best friends since they were children. "Sarah cried on the phone, your mother said, and claimed that Imogen is inconsolable, that you won't take her calls and you've even blocked her number."

Linc had a sudden desire to fling his snifter of brandy at the window behind his father's head. "Look, Dad. First, if Mother's so upset over my breakup, why didn't she call *me*?"

"She said she knew you wouldn't listen to her. I quote, 'Your son is as stubborn, selfish and intractable as his father.' It's always annoyed me when she speaks of me in the third person."

"I will call her and explain my position."

"I'm sure that will go well," his father muttered into his snifter.

"Dad, Imogen and I are over. Completely over.

She broke it off and I'm happy with that. I think it was the best thing for both of us."

His father sipped his brandy. Slowly. "So then what you're telling me is that you will not be coaxed or bullied into working things out with her."

"That is exactly what I'm telling you."

Warren's next words surprised him. "Good for you." He chuckled. "Don't look so shocked."

"Okay, Dad. I'm confused."

"Roll with it. As you know, I was never thrilled with Megan's decision to marry Kevin. Kevin was a nice man from an ordinary family. I knew that your sister could do better."

What did Kevin and Megan have to do with this? What was his father getting at here? Whatever it was, Linc felt bound to defend his dead brother-in-law. "Dad. Do you have any idea how insulting you're being to the memory of your own daughter— let alone the man himself? Kevin was a great guy."

"Of course, he was," Warren said wearily. "And he loved his wife and children. He also loved that ridiculous Cracker Jack box of an airplane and killed my daughter in the goddamn thing."

Linc tried not to imagine wrapping his fingers around his father's neck and squeezing. Hard. "Will you get to the point? Please."

"Gladly. Imogen was an imminently suitable wife for you. But it wouldn't have lasted."

"Isn't that pretty much what I already said?"

"It is. I'm agreeing with you. But frankly, in my

humble opinion, who says a marriage is supposed to last, anyway?"

"Dad. *I* do."

His father sipped his brandy. "Just like your sister, so sentimental. And back to my main point. Now that you have custody of my grandson and granddaughter, Imogen becomes an impossible choice as a wife for you. She's nothing short of a disaster in the making."

"How many times do we have to agree that we agree?"

His father just kept talking. "It's a matter of degrees. Were Megan and wannabe flyboy Kevin still alive, Imogen would have been perfectly acceptable for you. You would have spent fifteen or twenty years with her, during which you would never actually have been happy. But she would have given you children, which is what really matters. However, everything's changed now."

"And I'm assuming you're going to explain how?"

"Simple. Sarah Whitman's precious only daughter is much too self-absorbed to appreciate your sister's children."

Linc's head was spinning. "Wait. Just tell me. Why are you here if you think I've made the right decision in refusing to get back with her?"

"To be painfully honest, I had planned to bite the bullet and take your mother's side."

After a bracing sip from his own snifter, Linc prompted, "Because...?"

"I would like to make peace with Alicia."

"Why? You never see her or talk to her. She came back to the States for the funeral last January. I believe that's the only time she's ever been in Oregon since you divorced her."

"True, but I'm not getting any younger. I would like to feel that there's no animosity between me and my exes—and taking Alicia's part in this, speaking to you for her, seemed a way to get on her good side. I thought I would try to talk you into reaching out to Imogen and somehow making it work. But I didn't *like* having to do that."

"Because, as you've already said, Imogen wouldn't be good for Maya and Jayden?"

"Exactly. I'm not an especially affectionate man, as you know. Children make me nervous with their grabby little fingers and needy little hearts. Shelby says I'm going to need to work on that." Warren had a strange, bemused expression on his face. Before Linc could decide to ask him what that was about, he went on, "Shelby's right, of course. She almost always is. And I want my daughter's children to grow up safe, well cared for and happy, if possible. Jayden and Maya were never going to be happy with Imogen at your side. I felt guilty about that."

"But you were going to plead Mother's case for her, anyway?"

"Yes. But then I met the Bravo girl."

"Wait. Harper?"

"Yes, Harper."

"Meeting Harper changed your mind about trying to convince me to get back with Imogen?"

"That's right—though, to be honest, I'd already been having second thoughts about taking your mother's side on this, mostly because of Shelby. When I explained the situation to her and said I thought I'd found a way to make a stab at getting straight with your mother, my wife was not impressed with my plan. In fact, she was livid. She said that you had a right to make your own decisions about whom to love and marry and your mother and I needed to butt the hell out. Shelby is a bit of a sentimentalist, too, if you must know."

Warren and Shelby had met in Paris—at the world-famous bookstore, Shakespeare and Company. A whirlwind romance ensued. They'd married in Vegas eighteen months ago. Linc had only met his father's much-younger third wife briefly, last January, at the funeral. He remembered her as softly pretty, with lustrous brown skin, a thick cloud of natural curls and a warm smile. "Well. Good for Shelby, then."

"Yes, she is special and I miss her." Was that a dreamy expression on his father's face? Until this moment, Linc had never seen Warren Stryker looking dreamy about anyone. He found the sight vaguely disorienting. "Shelby refused to come to Portland with me because she didn't like my meddling in your situation vis-à-vis Imogen. Frankly, I can't wait to get back to her."

Linc got up and poured them each another brandy. When he took his seat again, he confessed, "I'm still confused, Dad."

"I can't say that I blame you."

"If meeting Harper changed your mind somehow, why even come back to talk to me now?"

His father stared into his snifter some more. "Did Harper tell you that I met her mother at Stanford?"

This conversation was giving Linc whiplash. "No. I'd barely gotten in the door when you rang at the gate. Harper did mention that you dropped by this morning."

Warren settled back against the cushions. "I have a confession to make."

"Okay...?" he replied with a slow, wary nod.

"I was completely taken with Marie Valentine all those years ago, as in struck by lightning, love at first sight. That kind of taken. Unfortunately, Marie wouldn't give me the time of day. She called me a supercilious prig." He shook his head. "I was crushed—and then furious a few years later when I learned she'd married some guy named Bravo from Texas. The Valentines are an old and respected Oregon family. I felt Marie could have done so much better."

Linc didn't know what to say. His father had once believed himself in love with Harper's mother? No way had he seen that coming. And he had no idea why Warren would tell him this now.

His dad seemed to shake himself. "In any case,

Harper looks so much like her mother. And it's obvious she has that same spirit, as beautiful inside as out. The children clearly adore her. She stood in the pool downstairs with Maya in her arms and Jayden hovering close and I thought, someone like her, that's who Lincoln ought to marry. Someone like Harper Bravo is going to love my daughter's children as much as her own. That was when I decided that not only would I *not* speak for your mother on the Imogen situation, I would come back this evening to tell you outright that I disagree with your mother. I hope that when you do marry, you choose someone who makes you happy, someone who will love not only your own children, but Maya and Jayden, as well."

Chapter Eight

"Did everything work out all right with your dad?" Harper asked two hours later.

By then, the kids were in bed and Linc was feeling pretty damn good.

And why wouldn't he feel good? He'd already made love to his favorite nanny twice—once hard and fast and a second time with slow and satisfying attention to detail.

He braced an elbow on his pillow and stared down at her, naked in his bed with that gorgeous wheat-colored hair like a wild halo around her arresting face. "You look so good in my bed."

She chuckled, a sweet, happy sound. "Why, thank you."

He traced a finger slowly from the center of her smooth forehead, down between her eyes, along the bridge of her nose, over those lush pink lips to her pointy, pretty chin. "My dad said you're as beautiful inside as out."

"Wow. I'm flattered."

"He likes you—and that's saying something. As a rule he reserves judgment on anyone until he's known them for decades, at least."

"What about his wife?"

"Shelby, you mean?"

"Yeah, his current wife. He can't have known *her* that long."

"You're right. He hasn't. And he appears to be completely in love with Shelby. Like you, Shelby's an exception to his general disdain for anyone he didn't go to school with. The jury's still out on whether he even likes *me*."

She shoved playfully at his bare chest. "That can't be true." Sliding her slim hand upward, she eased her fingers around his nape and rubbed gently.

He tipped his head back a little, encouraging her touch. It felt right, when she touched him. Already, he had trouble imagining his world without her to come home to.

She gazed up at him, those big eyes so direct, free of guile. "Warren told me that he'd met my mother in college."

"He mentioned that to me, too."

"Small world, huh?"

"Yes, it is." He bent for a kiss. Her lips parted in welcome. He took his time kissing her. When he lifted his head, she asked, "So, he just dropped by to say hi, then?"

Linc tried to decide how much to tell her. She'd made it much too clear that this thing between them was just for the holidays, that they were both supposed to move on when he and the kids returned to Portland. Would hearing that his dad thought he ought to marry someone like her have her leaping out of bed and reaching for her clothes?

Probably better not to mention it. And as for the whole mess with Imogen, well, that was the last thing he wanted to talk about right now.

He told the truth, just not all of it. "My dad was in town and knew I would be here for meetings. So yeah, he came by to check in with me."

"You didn't get much time together. Want to invite him for dinner tomorrow?"

God, no. "That's a nice thought. But he's heading back to Colorado tomorrow."

"So then he lives in Colorado now?"

"In Vail, yes. Shelby, his wife, grew up there. She owns and runs a bookstore and her parents are there."

Harper tugged on his earlobe. "I guess I won't suggest that you invite your dad and Shelby to Valentine Bay."

"They won't come."

"You won't know if you don't ask them."

"Let it go."

"Gotcha." She whispered, "Come down here."

He lowered his head till they were nose to nose. "What?"

"I think you have issues with your dad."

Smiling, he kissed her again. "Figured that out, did you?"

"Mmm-hmm."

"He's not so bad, really. And I meant what I said about him and Shelby. He's different since he met her—gentler. Kinder. The man is in love with his wife."

"You're saying he wasn't in love with your mom?"

"If he was, he never showed it much—same thing with his second wife, for that matter. I always thought he had no heart. It's possible I was wrong."

"So he's making progress, as a husband and a human being."

"That's one way to look at it, I guess. They do say that the third time's the charm." He rubbed his nose against hers and then nuzzled his way over her cheek to that perfect place behind her ear. From there, he carefully placed a line of kisses down the side of her silky neck.

She let out a soft, willing sigh.

And for the rest of the evening, Linc forgot all the troubling issues with his ex-fiancée. He gave no thought to his meddling mother or his suddenly rather likable father, who had once been in love—or at least deeply infatuated—with Harper's mother.

* * *

The next day, his meetings were shorter. He was able to get back to the house at a little after five. He and Harper took the kids out for pizza and then for a visit with Santa at Washington Square Mall.

Jayden was in his element. He perched happily on Santa's lap and talked the poor guy's ear off, posing for the photographer with a giant smile.

Maya was another story. She was fine at first, staring at Linc from Santa's knee, a little unsure of the concept, but willing to roll with it. The photographer snapped one shot of her, looking apprehensive.

And then she turned her head to glance up at the big guy in the red suit with the white beard.

"No!" she screeched and burst into frightened tears.

Linc scooped her back up again. She grabbed him around the neck, buried her face against his throat and wailed like it was the end of the world. He mouthed an apology at Santa and carried her back to where Harper waited.

"Hawp!" Maya cried, and reached for her, but without letting go of Linc. They ended up with both of them holding her, one of her little arms clutching each of them around the neck, the three of them all smashed together as she sobbed like the world was coming to an end, with Jayden standing close, staring up at them through worried eyes.

Slowly, Maya settled. Harper whipped out a tissue and wiped her tears away.

"I scawy," Maya whimpered, when the sobbing finally stopped.

Linc frowned at Harper, who translated, "Scary, I think—right, honey? You were scared?"

Maya sniffled and nodded.

"It's okay, Maya." Jayden tugged on her little pink shoe. "When you're scared of Santa, you can always try again next year."

Maya gave her brother a firm nod. "'Kay," she agreed.

Harper suggested, "I think right now what we all really need is ice cream."

Nobody disagreed with that. They went to Sub Zero, which made nitrogen-frozen ice cream to order. By the time they left the mall, Maya's fear of Santa had been forgotten, banished by a frozen concoction that included cookie dough, cake batter, chocolate syrup and sprinkles.

"Can we see the lights?" asked Jayden. "Please?"

It was a half-hour drive to Peacock Lane. They took the Marquam Bridge across the river to the Laurelhurst neighborhood in Southeast Portland.

Only a few of the pre-Depression-era houses on the four blocks that made up Peacock Lane had all their Christmas lights up this early in the season, but there were enough lavish displays to satisfy the kids. Linc drove slowly as the kids stared out the windows, happy and wide-eyed at the bright lights, the giant blow-up Santas, the prancing reindeer and waving snowmen.

The ride back to the house was a quiet one. Jayden and Maya dozed in the back seat. Linc played Christmas music on the Bluetooth, but down low. He and Harper didn't talk much, just shared a glance and a smile now and then.

He felt *connected* around her. Like everything made sense, all the random pieces of his life fitting together to make something good, something that felt so right.

So what if they'd only met a couple of weeks ago? Already he knew he needed to convince her to try Portland instead of Seattle when she made her move next year. Good thing he had the whole month to show her that she should be with him and he needed to be with her, and it shouldn't be that much harder for her to find satisfying work in his town.

That Sunday, he and the kids went with Harper up to Daniel Bravo's house for the regular Bravo family Sunday dinner. Jayden and Maya had a great time, trooping up and down the stairs after the older children, helping to set the tables when it was time to eat.

Linc enjoyed hanging out with Harper's family. They were a boisterous, fun crew. Being around them had him reflecting on how much he missed the sister he'd failed to spend enough time with while he'd still had the chance.

The Bravos also got him thinking about his dad, had him considering the possibility that maybe Warren Stryker wasn't such a poor excuse for a father, after all. He kept mentally revisiting Harper's suggestion that he invite his dad and Shelby to Valentine Bay sometime this month.

Tuesday at lunchtime, during a video chat with Alan and Jean, he mentioned that he'd seen his dad in Portland the week before.

Jean said, "I hope you got to spend some quality time with Warren. You don't see your dad enough."

He couldn't remember ever spending much time with his father—quality, or otherwise. "Well, he just stopped in for a drink Thursday evening, so we only had a little while together."

Alan said, "Megan used to reminisce on how your dad and your mother took you to Valentine Bay every Christmas, back when you and Megan were little."

"They did, yes."

"Why not invite him to the cottage?" Jean suggested. "You're in Valentine Bay for several weeks. He might find a time he can manage to fly out there."

It was so close to Harper's suggestion, he found himself replying, "I'll do that." And then instantly reconsidering. "Possibly…"

Jean smiled benignly. "Good, then. Think it over."

At which point, Maya held up Pebble and commanded, "Gamma, kiss-kiss." Jean blew a couple of big kisses, after which Jayden asked to see the ocean.

The giant ship was somewhere off the coast of

Guatemala at that point. Alan scooped up their laptop and carried it to a window of their penthouse stateroom so that Jayden could get a look at the view.

A few minutes later, as they were wrapping up the visit, Harper appeared.

Maya and Jayden greeted her with shouts of "Hawp!" and, "Harper! I drew more Christmas pictures!"

"Hi, Maya," Harper replied and then beamed at Jayden. "I can't wait to see those."

On the laptop screen, Alan and Jean shared a look. Jean asked, "Is that the nanny you hired?"

"It's Harper," Jayden corrected his grandmother.

Linc kind of loved that. Jayden saw Harper as a person, not a function. He signaled her over to sit with them on the sofa and made introductions as Maya crawled into Harper's lap and Jayden sprinted for the kitchen to grab the new pictures he'd stuck on the fridge.

Jean said, "It's such a pleasure to meet you at last."

Alan added, "We're glad you're there to help Linc look after the children."

"Me, too," replied Harper. "Your grandchildren are a lot of fun." She tipped her head to the side to make eye contact with the toddler in her lap. "Aren't you, Maya?"

"I fun!" cried Maya, and gave Pebble a hug.

Jayden came flying back in with his pictures.

Harper and the grands praised his work. "I think they're very festive," he proudly declared.

Jean said to Harper, "I hope we'll get to meet you in person one of these days. We won't be home from this trip until next summer. I don't know if Linc has told you that we live in the Sacramento area."

Harper nodded. "I think he mentioned that, yes."

"But they're thinking of moving to Portland," Linc couldn't resist putting in hopefully.

It pleased him no end when Alan backed him up. "Yes, we are," the older man said and added, for Harper's benefit, "Kevin was our only child…"

Jean sighed. "A beautiful, blessed, late-in-life baby." Her eyes were misty as she recalled her lost son. "And yes," she went on more briskly, "we're very seriously considering a move to Oregon, where we can be near the children and Linc."

"I'm holding you to that," Linc warned. Maybe he was pushing it, but he wanted them nearby. He'd grown attached to them in the past year. And it would be so good for the kids, to have their Grandma and PopPop dropping by often.

"Very seriously considering it," Jean repeated. "And lovely to get to chat with you a bit, Harper."

"Great to meet you, too."

Linc had to actively resist the need to hook an arm across Harper's shoulders, maybe steal a kiss—just on the cheek. A couple of simple, affectionate gestures that would let Alan and Jean know how important Harper had become to him.

But he had a feeling Harper wouldn't go for it. They were supposed to be keeping their relationship on the down-low around the kids. From Harper's point of view, his cuddling up to her in the biweekly video visit with the grandparents would be sending the wrong kind of signal.

They needed to talk about the future some more, him and Harper. And as soon as he found the right opening, they would.

After a flurry of kiss blowing and goodbyes, Jean and Alan signed off. Harper hustled the kids into their winter coats and drove them off to the theater for the afternoon rehearsal.

Linc went to his office, where for once there were no emergencies in Portland that needed to be dealt with immediately. He sat at his desk, trying to decide whether to check in with his assistant at Stryker Marine or start dealing with emails and messages, when his cell rang.

A glance at the screen had his stomach sinking.

It was his mother, whom he should have called days ago—ideally last Friday, after his talk with his dad on Thursday night. Or at least at some point over the weekend.

Yet here it was, the following Tuesday, and he was still putting off reaching out to her.

Well, not anymore.

He hit the talk button. "Hi, Mom. This is a surprise."

"Oh, I am sure that it is." Sarcasm dripped from every word.

He kept his tone light. "It's pretty late there, isn't it?"

"It's the middle of the night, Lincoln. The middle of the night and I can't sleep. That is very much due to you. Your father, who said he would talk to you, apparently gave you the wrong message altogether. After which, he got back to me and said *you* would be calling me. That was several days ago. Radio silence from you, thank you so much."

"Sorry, Mom." And he was. Sorry about a lot of things—including that he'd ever gotten involved with Imogen Whitman in the first place and that his mother was disappointed in her life and just generally unhappy. "I apologize for not calling. I did tell Dad I would get in touch with you. I should have done that days ago."

His mother let out a heavy sigh. "I just need to know when you are going to work things out with Imogen. Sarah is so upset and she says Imogen is miserable, longing to make it up with you. And yet you have refused to communicate with her. Lincoln, you *blocked* your own fiancée. I cannot believe you did that. I raised you better than that."

So much for keeping it light. "Look, Mom. There is no point in my communicating with Imogen. We broke up. I don't *want* to get back together with her."

"Lincoln, it's not all about you."

"It's 50 percent about me and *all* of me is through with Imogen."

There was more huffing from his mother. "I cannot believe you're doing this."

"Well, I am. And I'm sorry to be a disappointment to you, but your disappointment is not going to force me to marry a woman I don't love." At that, his mother gasped. He went on, calmly, "Marrying someone I don't love would be wrong and I think that you know it would."

"You made a promise."

"No, Mom. The promise happens when you stand up in front of the world and say, 'I do.' Imogen ended our engagement, thus saving both of us from making a promise we would only have broken eventually, anyway."

"She didn't *mean* to break up with you. She was upset and said things she regrets."

A headache had formed behind his eyes. Linc pinched the bridge of his nose between his thumb and forefinger and rubbed to ease the ache. He'd known this conversation was coming. But that didn't make having it any more bearable. "Look, Mom. This isn't about you. It isn't about Sarah. This is about Imogen and me and how it didn't work out. That's it. There's nothing more to say on the subject. You are not going to change my mind. So just give it up. Please?"

That seemed to silence her. But not for long. With

a hard huff of breath she demanded, "What am I going to say to Sarah?"

"I have no idea. The truth, maybe?"

"And what do you think is the truth? You have broken poor Imogen's heart."

"Mom, I think we've both said all we have to say on this subject. I don't want to talk about it anymore."

"Oh, that's just lovely. Stonewall me. You're just like your father."

He tried one more time to get through to her. "Let's talk about something else."

"No. This is important. We need to figure out a way for you and Imogen to—"

"Stop!" He didn't realize he'd practically shouted the word until he heard his mother gasp again. "I'm going to hang up now. Call me anytime, but not to talk about Imogen. I love you and I miss you. Goodbye."

"Don't you dare hang up on—" He disconnected the call, tossed the phone on his desk and dared it to ring again.

It didn't, but he flopped back in his chair and glared at it for several more seconds anyway, because when it came to his mother, he really had no idea how to get through.

Grabbing the phone again, he called his dad with the video-chat app.

Warren actually smiled at the sight of him. "Lincoln. What a surprise."

"Hey, Dad. I was just thinking about you, wondering if maybe you and Shelby might be able to make it out here to Valentine Bay for a Christmas visit this month? I would like to get to know Shelby a little. And Jayden and Maya should have a chance to know their grandpa on their mother's side."

Warren's brow beetled up. "I'll never be anyone's favorite grandfather."

"You don't have to be the favorite, Dad. But with grandkids, you really need to put in the time."

His father was quiet—until he said, "I'll check with Shelby."

"Excellent. We'll be here until January 2. Anytime between now and then works for me and the kids. Let me know."

At a little after five, Harper ushered Maya and Jayden in the front door. Jayden took off his hat and mittens and hung up his coat as he chattered away about how much he wanted it to snow.

Maya was exercising her independence. "*I* do. Me!" she insisted when Harper tried to help her out of her red puffer coat.

"Of course, you do," Harper replied. She planted a quick kiss on Maya's fat little cheek and stepped back to watch her take off her red-and-green beanie with the bouncing pom on top. Carefully, Maya set the beanie in the basket of hats and scarves by the door.

"How was rehearsal?"

Harper looked over to find Linc watching her from the open entrance to the living area. He had that look in those amber eyes, like he wanted to grab her and eat her right up. In three hours or so, he just might. A heated shiver skittered through her at the thought. "Never a dull moment," she replied.

"Ready for the big opening?" The Christmas show opening was four days away, on Saturday at two in the afternoon.

"Nope, we're not ready." She hung up her own coat. "But then, we never are."

"Hawp." Maya tugged on the hem of Harper's sweater. "Hewp."

"What do you say when you want help?"

The little girl's rosebud mouth curved in an angelic smile. "Pwease."

So Harper helped her out of her coat. Maya hung it up herself on the kid-height set of hooks above the basket of hats and scarves.

Three hours later, Harper let Linc lead her to his bed—by way of a long, lovely detour against the shut door of the master suite, where he knelt at her feet, hooked her left leg over his shoulder and then used his skilled fingers and clever mouth to send her to paradise.

Twice.

The man was amazing in so many ways.

Later, after another half hour of delicious love-making on the bed, Linc pulled the covers up.

Wrapped in the warm cocoon of blankets, with his arms around her, she asked him about his day.

He reported that he'd called his father and invited him and his wife to the cottage whenever they might be able to make it this Christmas.

"Did he say yes?"

"He's going to talk to Shelby."

She kissed his slightly stubbly jaw. "That's great."

He gave a grumbly sort of chuckle. "Proud of me, huh?"

"You'd better believe it—and I have to ask, what made you rethink the idea of inviting him?"

The question seemed to make him uneasy. "Uh. Long story…"

Chapter Nine

Again, Linc found himself debating how much to tell her.

But she knew him too well. "What's going on, Linc?"

He could definitely scare her off if he reported what had gone down with his messed-up mom, not to mention sharing the story of the ex who refused to let go.

But the woman in his arms had taught him a lot—about the children he had a sacred duty to shepherd into successful adulthood, about how families worked and what bound people together. He wanted more with her.

When the New Year came, he wanted her with

him. And to have any hope of convincing her that they should keep being together, he needed to be honest with her.

Her soft lips brushed the side of his throat. "Not going to tell me, huh?"

He lifted up enough to gaze down at her. "Just wondering where to start…"

"It can't be that bad. Come on now, lay it on out there."

So he did.

He told her everything: that his father had once had a thing for her mother and Marie Valentine had shut Warren Stryker down, that *his* mother was trying to get him to go back to his ex. He shared all the details, everything he'd been keeping to himself, even that his dad thought that he, Linc, ought to marry someone like her.

When he finally fell silent, she asked in a hushed voice, "Is that all?"

"Are you kidding? Isn't it enough?"

"I am not kidding, no. However, you're right. It's a lot."

"I just need to know you won't run away screaming now you have a better idea of the hot mess that is my family." He bent close and kissed her, thinking how she made everything better. One way or another, he needed never to let her go.

Was he moving too fast? Maybe. But losing Megan and Kevin had taught him that life could be brutal, brief and completely unfair. When a man found something really good, he needed to hold on to it.

She captured his gaze. "All families have issues. And I'm still right here in this bed with you, no plans to take off running."

He realized he'd been holding his breath. "Whew. That's what I needed to hear."

She studied his face. "Your mom sounds so unhappy…"

"She is—and pretty much always has been. I used to feel sorry for her, for the way my dad cheated on her and traded her in on a trophy wife. I still hate that he did that to her, but she's had years to deal with it, to move on, to make a life that works for her. And yet here we are, a decade later, and she's still an emotional disaster, more concerned over making Sarah Whitman happy than she is about creating a loving relationship with the grandkids she hardly knows."

"Or supporting *your* happiness," Harper suggested softly.

"Right. That, either."

Her eyelashes fluttered down. She became very engaged in not quite looking at him.

He tipped her chin up with a finger. "What? Just say it."

"Okay…" She hesitated, but then forged on. "It sounds like you and Imogen aren't really through."

"That's not true. It's over between her and me. I'm done."

"But *she* isn't."

"You're going to think I'm callous, but Imogen is my ex. It's over. That means she's not my problem."

She stared at him for a long time. But then at last, she nodded. "Okay, I get that. And you did explain to me before that you didn't love her—which is just sad, by the way."

"Yeah, it really is."

She took his face between her hands. "I see what you're saying. She wasn't the right person for you and you're glad that it's over."

"*Yes.* And can we leave this subject behind now?"

"All right."

"Thank you." He rolled to his side, taking her with him, so they were facing each other, eye to eye. "Well, that went pretty well."

"You think?"

"Hey, I just dumped a bunch of not-so-great information on you concerning me and my family— and you took it in stride."

Those beautiful dimples appeared. "The truth is hard to share sometimes."

On the nightstand, her phone pinged with a text.

He curled a silky swatch of her hair around his index finger. "You need to check that?"

At her half shrug, he reached over, picked it up and handed it to her.

She smiled as she checked the message. "It's just Mia."

"Of Acevedo Hybrid Homes?"

She rolled to her back again and thumbed out a reply. "Yeah. She and I keep in touch. I like her. We kid around, sending each other design problems—fun stuff, specific challenges that crop up when you work with shipping containers."

"So it's a design problem she just sent you?"

"Mmm-hmm." Stretching out an arm, she slid the phone onto the nightstand again. "She already has a solution, but she likes choices. So tomorrow morning I'll look over what she's sent and give her a few other ways she might go."

He pulled her into his arms again and kissed the tip of her nose. "They're missing the boat not hiring you before you run off to Seattle."

Now she frowned. "We've already addressed and dismissed that pipe dream."

It was far from the response he'd been hoping for. "It's not a pipe dream if it comes true."

"You just want me to come to Portland so we can keep spending our nights crawling all over each other."

"You are so right. I like what we have, and I do not want it to end."

Her serious expression became downright severe. "We have an agreement, Linc."

"We do. And part of our agreement is that things can change."

"I think…" Her pretty mouth twisted as she pressed on his chest with both hands.

"What? Say it."

"I, um, I think that, yes, you and I really like each other, and the sex is amazing, and I adore Jayden and Maya. And maybe you see this—you and me, together—as a way to make a more solid family for the kids."

Okay, that hurt.

Yeah, he did see her as a very good thing for his nephew and niece. But that was not the main point, no way. "You really think I want you as a nanny with benefits?"

"That's not what I said."

"Good. Because that's not what this is about. Yes, I love that you love the kids and that they feel the same about you. But that's not the reason I want to keep seeing you when the holidays are over. Harper, this is about you and me and this thing we have that I've never had before. It's about finally getting a taste of what being with the right person could mean. It's about not letting something special slip away when all the obstacles are surmountable."

She pressed two fingers to his lips and whispered, "It sounds so good when you put it like that."

"It's only the truth."

She held his gaze. "I have more I need to say."

"I don't want to hear how it can't work out for us." But she just kept staring at him, reproach in those big eyes. "Fine. Go ahead."

"I need you to see the other side of it, the part where I'm still trying to figure out who I am in this world and where I fit in. The fact that a few weeks ago, you were engaged to someone else. You and me, well, what if we're just a rebound for you? And what if, for *me*, we're only a distraction, an interlude—a way for me to avoid figuring out what to do with my life?"

"We're not."

"We can't let ourselves get all swept away in some romantic ideal, we can't go all insta-love and happy-ever-after about this."

Insta-love and happy-ever-after sounded pretty damn good to him. But he got that she needed practical solutions. "I'm not asking you to move in with me tomorrow. I just want a chance for us. I swear, if it were the least bit doable, I would relocate to Seattle. Unfortunately, Stryker Marine isn't all that portable."

"Linc, honestly. I'm not asking you to move to Seattle."

"And I need you to know that I've thought about it, that I've considered the possibility from every angle, but it's not going to happen anytime in the near future. And if *you* won't move to Portland, fine. Do what you need to do. Go to Seattle. It's not the other side of the world. With effort and planning, we can still see each other. We can see how it goes…"

Her eyes shone with moisture. "You seem so sure."

"I am sure. And I don't need for *you* to be sure—not yet. Right now, all I need is for you to stop saying no, to be open to trying to work things out."

With a soft cry, she grabbed him by the shoulders and yanked him down for a hard, hot kiss.

When they came up for air, he demanded, "Please

tell me you'll think about it, about you and me and more than just till New Year's, about the two of us deciding to find ways to be together, to build on what we've started this Christmastime."

Her beautiful mouth only trembled a little as she smiled.

"Tell me that smile means yes," he said gruffly.

She nodded. "Yes, I will be open to the possibilities."

"And we'll find ways to see each other after the holidays are over," he prompted.

"Yes. All right. After the holidays, we'll keep seeing each other."

"Exclusively," he added.

She nodded again. "Exclusively. Yes." And then she grinned at him. "Happy now?"

"It's a start."

The next morning, Linc woke to Jayden pounding on his bedroom door. "Uncle Linc! Get up. It's snowing!"

Linc rolled over and opened his eyes. The other pillow was empty. Harper had gone back to her place. He looked forward to the time when he could wake up every morning and find her there beside him.

He wasn't going to rush her, though. Last night, they'd made progress. He'd revealed some unpleasant truths, and she'd agreed that what they shared didn't have to end with the holidays. It was far from a promise of forever. But he would be patient with her. He'd asked for a chance with her and she'd said yes.

"Uncle Linc, come see!"

"Unc Wink, up! Now!" Maya chimed in from the monitor.

He shoved back the covers, pulled on some sweats and opened the door to an impatient little boy with small fists braced on his hips. "Finally." His irrepressible nature got the better of him and he dropped the stern expression. "Snow! We got snow!"

Linc ruffled his hair. "Come on. Let's get your sister up, put on our coats and go have a look."

In her room, Maya stood in her crib. She bounced up and down. "I wet!" she announced gleefully.

Linc changed her diaper and put her in warm leggings and a fluffy pink velour top. "Want to see the snow?" he asked as he hoisted her off the changing table.

"Yes!"

So they put on their coats and went out on the porch—where the snow was half rain that melted completely when it hit the ground.

Jayden refused to be disappointed. He predicted, "I just know we will get some by Christmas."

Linc made them breakfast and then hung out with them all morning. They were eating lunch when Harper arrived.

She entered the kitchen with pink cheeks and a halo of moisture clinging to her hair from the rain still coming down outside. "Wet out there," she said, and brushed at the crown of her head.

"The rain looks good on you," he replied, because it did. She gave him one of those smiles—the intimate kind, just between the two of them. "Everything looks good on you," he added.

And one way or another, he was going to make her see that they could have a future together. They only needed to reach out and take it.

Christmas on Carmel Street had its opening performance that Saturday afternoon. Linc brought the kids early. Harper was already there. He texted their arrival and she met him in the lobby. Taking Maya in her arms, she ushered Jayden backstage to get ready for the show.

Linc stood around in the lobby for a while, waiting for someone to take his five-dollar admission fee. Once that was handled, he entered the nearly empty auditorium. He chose a seat in the first row, so he would be ready to help with Maya if the need arose.

A few minutes after he sat down, Liam and Daniel Bravo, both of whom had kids in the show, appeared with their wives. The men sat on either side of Linc as Keely and Karin lingered in the aisle to chat. The men talked about the Blazers, the Seahawks and the Christmas show the year before. Liam and Daniel agreed that the kids loved being part of it. A few minutes before showtime, Keely and Karin took seats beside their husbands.

By the time the curtain went up, there wasn't an empty seat in the house. The children were all on their best behavior, earnest and serious even when they missed an entrance or forgot a line. Prompters from the wings on either side of the stage kept things on track.

The audience of parents and grandparents and doting aunts and uncles seemed to love every minute of it. Linc certainly did. Maya played an angel in two of the biggest musical numbers. A girl of twelve or thirteen seemed to have been assigned to keep an eye on her. The girl held Maya's hand and whispered to her now and then. Maya never once froze up or fussed. Linc was so proud of her.

As for Jayden, he kept popping up in every other scene. He played an angel, too. He was also one of Santa's reindeer, a little drummer boy, a nutcracker and a singing, dancing squirrel.

As he pranced around in his squirrel costume, Daniel leaned in and whispered, "Kid's got talent."

Linc thought of Megan. His heart ached, missing her, wishing he could look over and see her, right there beside him, beaming in pride at her daughter and son.

After the standing ovation and extended curtain calls, Linc would have gone backstage to heap praise on his niece and nephew. But just about every other adult in the audience seemed to have the same idea.

He skipped the pandemonium back there and waited in the lobby. The place had pretty much

cleared out by the time Harper emerged, holding
Jayden's hand on one side and Maya's on the other.

The kids ran to him. He bent to gather them into
a group hug. Jayden chattered away, excited at his
success, with Maya interjecting, "I so good!" or "I
happy!" every time her brother paused for a breath.

Linc told them how wonderful they were, glancing up now and then at Harper, who stood a few feet
away wearing busted-out jeans and one of her big,
floppy sweaters, that yellow puffer coat flung over
one shoulder. She had her hair piled up in a sloppy
bun, her face scrubbed clean of makeup. Never in
his life had he seen a woman more beautiful.

"We should get ice cream to celebrate," he offered, when the pint-size thespians had settled down
a little.

They all agreed that was a great idea. Holding
hands, they walked up the street to a shop called
Scoopy Do's. It was almost five when they got back
in the car. Maya snoozed on and off during the ten-
minute ride to the cottage. Jayden was still flying
high, singing along to the Christmas tunes on the
Bluetooth, reminiscing about his favorite moments
in the show, announcing that he could hardly wait
for their second performance next Saturday.

At the house, Linc and the kids helped Harper
make dinner. After that, they hung out in the living area, enjoying the tree and the fire. It was a
great night.

And it only got better. Once the kids were in bed,

he and Harper went to his room. She stayed until one in the morning. He tried to convince her to sleep over, but she insisted she really did have to go, so he put on some sweats and followed her downstairs for a kiss at the door.

"Text me when you get to your place."

She kissed him again, a quick one. "I know the drill."

"You really should just stay over. There's no need for you to go wandering around in the dark late at night."

She put a finger to her lips. "Good night, Linc." And she slipped out the door.

He stood there alone in the foyer, missing her already, though she'd just left. It wasn't long before his phone pinged with a text.

Home safe.

Come back.

I will. Tomorrow.

I'm so lonely without you.

He added a crying face emoji just to drive his point home.

Yes, he was a grown-ass man who'd always found emojis ridiculous. But then Harper Bravo entered his life, lighting him up with all the warm, fuzzy, gooey feelings he hadn't realized could be so satisfying.

In response to his emoji, she sent him a GIF of two teddy bears hugging in a rising cloud of pink and red hearts and a reply of:

Good night, Linc.

He still wished she'd stayed, but he went back upstairs smiling.

As for the week that followed, it was pretty close to perfect. Twice, he caught Harper texting with Mia Acevedo. Was he growing more and more certain that Mia would offer her a job?

You bet he was. He considered calling Mia, casually suggesting that Acevedo Hybrid Homes ought to hire Harper, maybe even discussing how he could help if the company needed an investor before they would be ready to take on a second designer.

He never made that call and probably never would, not without getting Harper's okay first. She'd made it painfully clear that she didn't want him butting in, that no way would she take a job he'd arranged for her. He didn't agree with her on that, but he respected her determination to do it on her own.

Saturday brought the second and final performance of *Christmas on Carmel Street*. There were more gaffes than last week, but the audience response was every bit as enthusiastic as before.

After the curtain calls, the Valentine Bay Community Club served coffee, punch and cookies in the lobby. They were trolling for donations to the arts council, which sponsored the events in the theater. Linc whipped out his black card and contributed.

Early Sunday, he put the kids in the Rover, picked up Harper at her cottage and they all four returned to the theater to help strike the Christmas show set. Linc and Harper took turns keeping Maya entertained and out of the way of the busy workers. In the afternoon, they drove up Rhinehart Hill to Daniel's for the family meal and ended up staying later than usual.

It was after five when they headed back home, with Jayden providing a running commentary about how fun the afternoon had been and Maya, as usual, dropping quickly off to sleep.

The twisting driveway to the cottage was lined with tall trees. Oregon grape and giant, close-growing ferns filled the gaps between the thick trunks. The house didn't come into view until they were almost upon it—which meant Linc didn't see the Lexus parked in the open space near the porch until the very last turn.

Jayden spotted the unfamiliar car about the same time Linc did. "We got company," the little boy said.

The driver's door opened and a good-looking middle-aged woman in wide-legged gray wool pants, high-heeled suede boots and a pale pink wool coat that flowed to midcalf got out. She carried a designer purse the size of a bowling bag and, though it was already dark out, she wore giant sunglasses pushed up on the top of her head.

She was the last person Linc had ever expected

to see at the cottage—or anywhere in Oregon, for that matter.

He glanced at Harper. She gave him a shrug. Apparently, she assumed that he was as much in the dark about their visitor as she was. "Don't ask me. I have no idea who that might be."

"It's my mother," he said.

Chapter Ten

"At last!" his mother exclaimed when he pushed open his door and got out of the Rover. "I've been waiting for hours." He met her midway between the two vehicles. She offered her cheek for a kiss, which he dutifully provided.

"This is a surprise." He pulled his phone from his pocket to check messages. She hadn't texted, called or emailed. "I had no idea you were here—or that you were coming."

"I confess." Swiftly, she peeled off her driving gloves and shoved them into a pocket of her coat. "I wanted to surprise you."

I'll bet. "Well, Mom. You did."

She put her hand against his cheek. Her smooth

fingers were cold. "So good to see you, darling." Her fond smile seemed strained. And why wouldn't it be? There was only one reason she would fly here from Italy without saying she was coming. She intended to confront him about Imogen face-to-face. "Merry Christmas."

"Merry Christmas, Mom."

Harper's door opened at the same time as Jayden's.

His mother ignored Harper and focused on Jayden as he climbed from the vehicle. "Jayden Michael, I swear you've grown a foot since last January. Come here this instant and give your grandmother Alicia a hug."

Jayden went right to her. "Hi, Grandma," he said politely, and submitted to the hug. Linc's chest constricted at the sight. Jayden recognized his mother's mother, but nothing more. She was a virtual stranger to him.

In the meantime, Harper had taken Maya from her car seat. The little girl yawned and rested her head on Harper's shoulder.

Alicia, her eyes narrowed now, finally looked at Harper—but only to issue a cold command. "Let me see Maya."

Harper carried the half-asleep toddler around the front of the Land Rover.

Alicia stared fixedly at Harper. "Hello." Her mouth tipped up at the corners—but barely.

Linc made the introductions. "Harper Bravo, my

mother, Alicia Buckley." His mother had taken her maiden name again after the divorce.

"It's a pleasure." Harper looked uncomfortable, but she managed to inject warmth into the words.

Apparently, Alicia had forgotten all about the little girl snoozing on Harper's shoulder. "You're a local?"

Harper smiled a gentle smile. "I am, yes."

"Ah. I wasn't aware that Linc had local—" she paused just long enough to make the final word of the sentence an insult "—friends."

Linc jumped in before his mother could embarrass him further. "I *do* have friends here in Valentine Bay. Harper has the next cottage over. She and her sister Hailey direct and produce the community Christmas show. Both Jayden and Maya performed in the show this year. You missed a treat, Mom. I wish you'd let me know that you were coming."

"I'm sure you do," Alicia replied sourly.

Maya lifted her head and squinted up at Harper. "Hawp. Hungwy." She rubbed at her sleepy eyes.

Alicia suddenly remembered that she'd been ignoring her only granddaughter. She loomed in close. "Hello, Maya Renee. Do you remember me?"

Still half-asleep, Maya frowned at the strange woman with the sunglasses on her head. Then she turned to Harper and asked again, "Hungwy?"

"It's been a while since we ate." Harper sent Linc a speaking look. He wasn't sure of the exact meaning, but he got the general drift. His mother was behaving badly and Harper didn't know what to do with that. "A snack wouldn't hurt." She held out her hand to Jayden. "Let's go in." The little boy darted right to her and slipped his fingers in hers. "Nice to meet you." She gave Alicia a much cooler smile than the previous one and turned for the steps.

Linc resisted the need to get right in his mother's face about her rudeness to Harper. Later for that, though. First things first. "Pop the trunk, Mom. I'll get your bags."

Alicia had the keyless remote in her hand, but she didn't use it. She waited until Harper and the kids went inside to demand, "What is she, the house-keeper?"

Linc answered flatly, "Her name is Harper, in case you weren't paying attention—Harper Bravo. And no, Harper is not the housekeeper. Pop the trunk."

Alicia punched a button on the remote and the trunk sailed up. "Is there something going on be-tween you and that girl?"

It was too much. "I had forgotten how rude you can be—and to answer your question, yes. There is. Harper is important to me. She matters. If you have any consideration for me at all, you will treat her with respect."

Alicia drew her shoulders back and spoke in a silky, even tone. "I'm your mother. I love you and want the best for you. I've come all the way out to the edge of the Pacific Ocean to get you to see what a horrible mistake you're making."

He considered suggesting she find a hotel. At least then he wouldn't have to deal with all her ugly shit. But he couldn't quite make himself kick his own mother to the curb. "What did I say the last time we spoke?"

"Is this a quiz?" she chirped aggressively.

"If you're coming in—"

"Of course, I'm coming in."

"Great. You will treat Harper with courtesy and kindness."

"Of course I will, Lincoln."

"And you will accept that Imogen and I are through."

"But I don't accept that."

"Then there's no point in your coming inside."

That set her back a fraction. "You don't mean that."

"Make up your mind, Mom."

She actually teared up. "I am so frustrated with you."

"Same. Make up your mind."

Alicia took off the sunglasses, put them back on and slid them up on top of her head again. "All right. I will say nothing more about you and poor Imogen."

He drew a slow, deep breath. "Good. How long are you staying?"

She put her hand to her mouth and then to her throat. "A few days?"

"Fair enough, then." He went around to the open

trunk and pulled out a pair of floral-themed Gucci suitcases. "It's good you're here. You can get to know your grandchildren a little."

Linc made certain to be standing in the hallway outside Jayden's door when Harper emerged after tucking him in.

She shut the door and turned to him. Her beautiful face had *I've got to get out of here* written all over it. "I think I should probably—"

"Stay."

She leaned in close and lowered her voice to a near whisper. "Your mother—"

"—is jet-lagged. She's gone to her room for the night. She won't be bothering us."

"Linc, come on. She doesn't like me. I just need a little space, that's all."

As far as he knew, Alicia had been civil, at least. But maybe she'd crossed the line at some point while his back was turned. If she had, he would get her a hotel room—tonight, if possible. "What did she say to you?"

That plump mouth twisted into a tight frown. "Look. It's not any particular thing that she said. It's just very clear to me that she doesn't want me here."

"She's messed up. She took a position as wronged and wounded when my father divorced her—and she *was*, on both counts. He was having an affair with his assistant at Stryker Marine while he and my mother were still married. Then he divorced my mother and married the woman he'd cheated on her with. She was deeply and understandably hurt by his betrayal, and also by the humiliation of being traded in on a younger model. But since then, she hasn't moved on. It's like she got stuck there, being the injured party."

"I just don't want to be in the middle of it."

"Harper, you have to see that my mother's issues are not your fault. Please don't let her chase you away."

"I'll be back tomorrow. But for tonight, I think it would be easier if I went home."

"What it would be is giving in. And giving in to my messed-up mother solves nothing."

She sagged against the wall by Jayden's bedroom door. "She came all this way to see you and the kids…"

He moved in closer, wanting to soothe her, needing to convince her to stay. "No, she didn't." The words were out before he stopped to think that they would require an explanation—and that explaining the real reason Alicia had shown up on his doorstep would not make Harper any more willing to stay.

"If she didn't come to see her son and her grandchildren, then why…?" The sentence met an untimely death as she put it together. "Omigod. Imogen. Is she here to talk you into getting back with your fiancée?"

"*Ex*-fiancée." And wait. Had he just admitted that Harper was right? He wanted to slap a strip of duct tape on his own damn mouth—but then again, she would have figured it out eventually, anyway. And she would not have been pleased that he'd put off telling her. He captured her hand before she could take off down the stairs. "Let's go to my room. We'll talk about this. Please."

She didn't look happy, but she did let him lead her along the hallway and into the master suite. Once he had her in his private space, he shut the door and turned the lock. She headed straight for the sitting area. Dropping to the sofa, she grabbed a throw pillow and hugged it to her chest as though to shield herself from whatever difficult truth he might be about to throw at her next.

At least she toed off her chukka boots and gathered her feet up to sit cross-legged on the cushions. "Okay. I'm here. What's going on?"

He made himself lay it out there. "I've ended my relationship with my mother's longtime best friend's daughter, and now my mother is determined I'm not going to do to Imogen what my father did to her."

"But the two situations are not the same."

"Exactly. But as I've said before, my mother is screwed up."

She gave him a long, unhappy look and then said, "What does your mother know about you and me?"

He didn't quite dare to sit next to her, so he took the club chair across the low table. "What do you mean, 'what does she know'?"

"Really, Linc? I have to ask all the individual

questions?" She tossed the pillow to the sofa—and then picked it right back up and hugged it again. "Will you please just explain to me what the heck is going on here?"

"I, erm, implied to my mother that we're together."

"You *implied*?"

"I didn't know how far to go. You've been pretty damn clear that we're not rushing into anything. I said that you mean a lot to me and she'd better treat you with respect."

A rush of color flooded up her neck and over her cheeks. "You *threatened* her—you threatened your *mother*?"

Adrenaline burned through him. Why was he the bad guy in this? "I said she couldn't stay here if she wasn't going to be civil to you and that I expected her to accept that Imogen and I are through. I said if she couldn't agree to those two conditions, I would find a hotel for her to stay in."

Slim shoulders slumped. "You threatened her. No wonder she hates me."

"She doesn't hate you."

"Oh, please. I've spent most of the evening in proximity to her. If her looks could kill, I would not be breathing."

"Harper…"

Her back snapped up straight again. "Does she know I'm the temporary Christmas nanny?"

"Harper—"

"Please answer the question."

"No, she doesn't know."

At that, Harper slapped the pillow against her face and groaned into it. He knew he was just about to lose her. But then she put the pillow down and groaned again—a softer groan this time. "Now I don't know *what* to do. I can't figure out which is worse, her thinking I'm the help—which is true, actually—or her thinking I'm some gold-digging local yokel chasing a rich potential sugar daddy, watching the kids and hanging around here all the time trying to worm my way into your good graces."

"Stop. You are much more than the help, and we both know it. And you know damn well you don't have to knock yourself out to get near me. The two of us can't get close enough, as far as I'm concerned. I mean it. You can't buy into her garbage."

Her cheeks puffed out with a hard breath. "She's your *mother*. I don't want her to hate me."

He got up and went to her. Sweet relief loosened the knots in his belly when she didn't pull away. Instead, she made room for him, shifting and tucking her legs to the side so that he could sit next to her. Better still, she didn't object when he pulled her into his arms. "Please don't get torn down about her."

"Oh, Linc…" She leaned against him and rested her head on his shoulder. "This is awful."

He pressed his cheek to the crown of her head and breathed in the lemony scent of her hair. "She's completely unreasonable. I don't know what to do with her. I think the best move is that tomorrow, I'll just tell her she can't stay here."

Harper tipped her head back to meet his eyes. "No. That would be wrong. I think we have to be gentle and direct with her."

He gave a pained chuckle. "Like we are with Maya and Jayden?"

"Yeah, pretty much. And we have to just tell her that we're a couple."

We're a couple.

Hallelujah! She'd actually said it.

Suddenly, in spite of everything, the world was a beautiful place. "Say that again." He couldn't keep the giant smile from stretching across his face.

"Well, I mean, we're not putting labels on what we have, but we *are* together." She looked so sweet and earnest. He wanted to kiss her. He wanted to make love to her. Most of all, he wanted to keep her. Forever, if possible.

Somehow, in less than four short weeks, he couldn't picture his life without her in it. Not anymore. Never again.

"Right?" she prompted.

He nodded for all he was worth. "Yes. No doubt. We are together."

"We have to say it, though. We have to tell your mother that we're together and that you're paying me to help you look after the kids until you go back to Portland. I think we need to just put it all out on the table, let her make whatever she wants to make of it. Hiding stuff from her is only going to come back to haunt us later."

"I love it when you say 'us.'" He closed his eyes and drew in a slow breath. "However, given the way she's been behaving, it just feels like anything we say about our relationship will only be handing her more ammunition, giving her more opportunities to wreak havoc."

Harper pulled away. "What's she going to do—tell Imogen?"

"Yes—or she'll tell her BFF, Sarah, who happens to be Imogen's mother, and then Sarah will tell Imogen."

"But, Linc, is there a reason we should care that Imogen knows about you and me?"

If Imogen scares you away? Absolutely, he thought. He said, "God, no. We should not care. *I* don't care."

"Well, okay then. Can we agree that we have a plan? That we'll treat your mother with kindness. We'll tell her exactly what we are to each other and refuse to be intimidated by her bad behavior because we are doing nothing wrong."

"Agreed." But he had to say it. "Though I'm afraid she's still going to do everything in her power to make you want to run away screaming."

"Yeah. That won't be fun. But family matters, Linc. It's important that you do your best to get along with her."

He wasn't so sure. "I understand why you believe

that. I've met *your* family. They're worth knocking yourself out for."

"All families are." Now those big eyes had turned pleading. "Linc. She's your *mother*. I couldn't stand to be the reason you aren't speaking to her."

"You are not and will never be the reason." He stroked a hand down the vibrant silk of her hair, wanting to soothe her, to get her to see that sometimes everything is *not* going to come out right. "She's impossible. I'll try to make it work with her, for your sake. But I'm only going to take so much of her bad behavior. Sometimes, even with family, a guy's got to draw the line."

As usual, Harper left around midnight.

The next morning, Alicia slept late.

Linc got up bright and early with Jayden and Maya. His mother had yet to emerge from the guest room upstairs when Linc's dad called.

"That invitation still open?" Warren asked. "Shelby and I were thinking of flying out there tomorrow. We'll charter a jet and fly into that little airport right outside town. We won't stay long, just overnight, arriving in the afternoon tomorrow and taking off around lunchtime Wednesday. I'm thinking I need to see Jayden and Maya, and I want to put something under the tree for each of them."

Linc hesitated. He couldn't help but be torn between how pleased he was that his father was making an effort—and how his mother would take being under the same roof with her cheating ex and his third wife.

"The silence on your end is deafening, son." Warren sounded vaguely amused.

"Sorry. I do want you to come. Full disclosure, though. Mom's here."

A beat, then starkly, "You're not serious."

"Yes, I am." Linc glanced across the living room, where Maya lay on the floor cuddling her stuffie, Pebble, and staring contentedly up at the Christmas tree. Jayden was up in his own room, where he couldn't overhear this conversation. Linc lowered his voice, anyway. "Mom's on the warpath over my breakup with Imogen."

Warren said something under his breath. "You also realize I'm not on her good side."

As if that was news. "I assumed as much."

"Are you sure you still want us to come?"

"I'm sure. Just as long as you know it probably won't be all that pleasant dealing with her."

"No it won't. And I have to update Shelby on this development before we confirm."

"I get that."

"Hang on?"

"I'll be here."

Two minutes later, Warren was back. "All right. You asked for it. We'll see you tomorrow."

"That's great, Dad." He realized he meant it. "I'm glad you're coming."

"Just one more thing you really should know…"

"Sure."

"You're going to have a baby sister. Shelby's pregnant. We're seven months along."

Alicia came out of her room at a little after eleven. She went straight to the coffee maker in the kitchen. Linc considered following her in there to give her a heads-up on Warren and Shelby's visit *and* to let her know that Harper was his girlfriend and the temporary nanny.

But then he thought better of that. Alicia was just too likely to behave badly when he laid the news on her. The kids didn't need to witness their grandmother in a meltdown.

He would have a talk with her this afternoon when Harper would be here to look after Maya and Jayden. Or maybe tonight, after the children were safely tucked in their beds.

Alicia fixed herself a late breakfast and returned to her room. When Harper arrived at one, Linc was sprawled on the sofa across from Jayden, who sat cross-legged on the floor, hard at work on another Christmas work of art, using the coffee table as his workspace.

"Look, Harper." He held up his creation for her approval as she entered the room. "It's Santa by the tree."

She went right to him. "I love it."

"I do, too," he agreed, and then put the paper

down on the coffee table again, grabbed a red crayon and bent to his work.

Maya toddled over to her from her favorite spot beside the tree. "Up, Hawp!"

Harper scooped his niece into her arms and turned to Linc with a smile that made everything better. She asked, "Where's your mother?"

"Upstairs in her room." She hadn't come down since she went up there after her late breakfast.

"Kiss," commanded Maya and stuck her stuffie in Harper's face.

Harper laughed, kissed Pebble and then asked, "Did you get a chance to talk to her?"

"I thought I would wait until you were here to keep an eye on the kids."

She nodded. "Good idea."

"There's more. My dad and his wife are coming tomorrow, just for overnight. Shelby's pregnant."

Harper grinned. "Go, Warren!"

And then both of them were laughing. It was all just too weird, like they were living in a soap opera.

Maya asked, "Funny?"

When both Harper and Linc nodded, she laughed, too.

Harper said, "I think I'll take the kids back to my cottage. We'll work on our homemade Christmas presents."

"Pwesents!" crowed Maya. She was a big fan of those.

Harper added the unfun part. "You can talk to her while we're gone."

Twenty minutes later, Harper and his niece and nephew set out for the Bravo cottage. Linc climbed the stairs in dread.

"Come in," his mother answered, so polite, cold as ice, when he tapped on her door.

He pushed it open and found her sitting in the corner chair, reading glasses perched on her nose and a book open in her lap. "Got a minute?" he asked.

"Certainly." She marked her place and set the book aside.

He crossed the threshold and closed the door behind him. "Just a few things I think you ought to know…"

She gave him a half-hearted smile that came off more as a grimace. "All right."

He had no clue of the right way to begin, so he just started talking. In five sentences, he got out everything he'd come upstairs to say to her. Lamely, he finished with, "So that's about it."

The look she gave him probably should have sliced him in half, but all it did was make him feel weary to the core. "All right, then. To recap. Your father is coming. His third wife, the child bride, is pregnant, and this Harper person, who is *not* your fiancée and whom you are paying to look after my daughter's children, just happens to be your girlfriend." Acid burned each word as it fell from her lips.

Get the hell out.

He wanted to say it so bad he could taste it.

But again he reminded himself that Harper wanted him to try to get along with her. "That's about the size of it," he said flatly.

"This is outrageous."

And that about did it for him. "I'm done with your crap, Mom. I'm sorry your life didn't pan out the way you wanted it to. But that's just not my fault—nor is it Harper's fault."

"That girl is—"

"Amazing and warm and wonderful and the best thing that ever happened to me—*and*, did I mention, my sister's children adore her? I'm going to do everything in my power to convince her to keep seeing me after Christmas is over. And I've got to tell you, Mom. You are not helping. You show up here without letting me know that you're coming and all you do is stir up trouble. I've had enough of your seething looks and your unacceptable attitude and your complete lack of interest in your dead daughter's wonderful children. I'm not putting up with any more of it. I want you to leave."

She rose. He waited for her to refuse to go and wondered what the hell he was going to do then.

But it didn't come to that. She merely shrugged. "Have it your way, Lincoln. I'll be out of here within the hour."

Chapter Eleven

"I notice the Lexus is no longer out front," Harper said mildly when she and the kids came back from the other cottage.

Linc stuck his hands in his pockets. "Yeah. We had a little talk. My mother decided it was time to go."

Jayden hooked his coat on a low peg by the door and turned to Linc, frowning. "Grandma Alicia left?"

"Yes," Linc replied. "She said to tell you goodbye and she hoped to see you soon." Alicia had said no such thing and he shouldn't be lying to his nephew. On the other hand, why the hell did an innocent five-year-old have to feel as bad as Linc did right now?

Answer: he didn't. And Linc had no qualms about doing whatever it took to make sure he wouldn't.

Jayden seemed puzzled. And why shouldn't he be? His grandmother had blown in and rushed out, and while she was here, the only attention she'd paid to him had lasted all of two seconds when she first arrived. Jayden suggested in a wary tone, "Maybe she can come for my birthday."

"Maybe," Linc agreed as noncommittally as possible.

"We'll talk later," Harper said to Linc.

"Yeah," Linc replied, feeling guilty that he'd driven his mother away—even though he would do it all over again in a heartbeat, given the same situation.

"I *do* it. Me!" Maya announced proudly. Linc glanced down at her. Totally oblivious to the disappearance of her maternal grandmother, Maya had taken her coat off all by herself and hooked it on a low peg beside Jayden's.

"Great job!" Harper dropped to a crouch, pulled the little girl close and blew a raspberry against the side of her neck.

Maya erupted in a fit of giggles and Linc felt better about everything.

That night, when the kids were in bed and he and Harper were alone in Linc's room, he explained what had happened with Alicia.

Harper took it well, he thought—and that was another thing he loved about her. The way she rolled with the punches. She'd tried to get him to be patient with his mother. But once he'd had enough, she didn't jump his ass for asking Alicia to leave.

She also didn't say one bad word about his mother, though Alicia had treated her coldly, dismissed her as "the help," and disparaged the relationship he and Harper were creating together.

"Come here." He pulled her into his arms and kissed her.

She kissed him back as they undressed each other.

One kiss led to another—slow, intense, drugging kisses that went on forever and yet somehow were never quite long enough.

He guided her down to the bed and kissed his way along her soft, gorgeous body, settling in at the sweet spot between her sleek thighs. He could stay here forever, making love to her with his mouth and his stroking hands, as if they never had to get out of this bed for the rest of their lives.

Later, inside her, so deep and so right, he stared into her eyes and longed to just say it, *I love you, Harper Bravo.*

But now wasn't the time. He got that. He did. She had changes she needed to make, a new career to create. For her, it was too early to speak of love and sharing the rest of their lives.

And he could wait for as long as she needed him to wait. For as long as it took her to realize what he already knew—that she was smart and eager and focused and willing to put in the time. One way or another, she would find the kind of work that fulfilled her.

But she wouldn't believe him just because he said it. She needed to prove it for herself.

After the unpleasantness with Alicia, Harper wasn't sure what to expect of the visit from Linc's father and stepmother.

Warren and Shelby arrived in a rented red Escalade. Linc and Harper and the kids went out to greet the newcomers.

Warren was pretty much as Harper remembered him from that brief encounter at the indoor pool in Linc's Portland house a couple weeks before. Cool, distant and faintly amused at the sight of his grandchildren, Warren greeted Harper with an aloof smile and a surprisingly sincere sounding, "Lovely to see you again."

But when he wrapped his arm around his wife and introduced her to Harper, a whole other side of the man appeared. With his twenty-six-year-old pregnant bride, Warren Stryker was smiling and attentive and so clearly in love.

Seeing them together, Harper felt she understood Linc's dad at least a little bit better. He might have made a mess of things in a whole bunch of ways, but he'd finally found the right woman for him. Now, he was a happy man. And Harper could understand why.

Shelby, petite and very curvy with a giant baby bump, had a big, openhearted laugh and a smile that could put just about anyone at ease. Within ten minutes of entering the cottage, she had Maya in her arms and Jayden following her around, asking her a lot of questions and not waiting for the answers.

They all spent a couple of hours hanging around the cottage with the Christmas tunes playing. Shelby insisted the kids open one of the many presents she and Warren had brought. It was a simple board game called Little Garden. Players had to help Gardener Gabriel build the garden before Molly Mole ate all the fruits and vegetables. Even Maya could play. They all joined in, Warren, too, though a bit reluctantly.

They had dinner at the table in the dining room. Shelby raised her glass of sparkling cider in a toast to family and the holidays.

The kids were in bed by a little after eight and the adults sat in the living area for a while, the talk easy and casual.

Shelby explained that she'd taken over her family's bookstore right after she graduated from the University of Southern California with a business degree. "I planned to go on to study law. But my dad had some health problems. I went home to Colorado and started running the bookstore for him. What can I say? I loved it. My parents are my partners. We bought the shop next door, tore out the adjoining wall and now we have a bookstore café. Profits are up and we're opening a second store in Denver."

She said that she'd met Warren nearly two years before on her first trip to Europe.

"It was love at first sight," added her husband.

Shelby laughed her full-out, beautiful laugh. "Not exactly."

Warren conceded, "Fine. I was too old for you—meaning I was only a few years younger than your mother, and your mother did not want her brilliant only daughter marrying a twice-divorced, white senior citizen."

"You are fifty-seven," said Shelby. "Too young to qualify as a senior citizen—and we both know that my mama never said any such thing."

Warren didn't argue. "Whatever you say, my darling."

Shelby leaned his way and kissed his cheek. "Notice how he says he *was* too old for me. Past tense?"

Warren's smile was nothing short of smug. "It's a fact. Love makes a man young. And youth comes on swiftly. The younger I got, the more willing you became to accept that we were meant to be together. And then, after you realized I was the only man for you, I still had my work cut out for me convincing Louella."

"That's my mama," Shelby clarified.

"And she did come around," said Warren.

Shelby chuckled. "It didn't take that long."

"No, but it *felt* like forever until you were mine." Warren took his wife's hand. "Finally, Shelby said yes."

Shelby turned a benign smile on Linc and Harper. "It was two months from the day we met in Paris to that Vegas wedding chapel with the minister who looked way too much like Elvis."

Warren took her hand. "From the moment I met you, every hour without you was pure torture." They interwove their fingers and leaned in for a quick kiss.

Harper glanced Linc's way and found him already looking at her. His mom might be a nightmare, but Harper really liked Warren and Shelby. It seemed to her that Linc was thinking pretty much the same thing.

She felt warm all over and couldn't help longing to take a chance on what they had together, to go for it with Linc, agree to move to Portland, follow her heart instead of her need to get out there and prove herself as a functioning adult.

A few minutes later, Warren brought up the elephant in the room. "So then, Lincoln. Your mother isn't here. What happened?"

Linc glanced away. "Yeah, she left early. I asked her to go."

Warren frowned. "You have that look, son. The one that says you don't want to talk about it."

"You're right. I don't."

"Then we won't. But if there's anything I can do—"

"I don't see what."

Warren gave a slow nod. "I understand. I'll let it go."

They sat in silence for a minute or two as Willie Nelson crooned "Pretty Paper" from the speaker on a nearby table. Harper sternly reminded herself that she had important goals to achieve and she couldn't afford to get too wrapped up in fantasies about her and Linc and happily-ever-after.

As the song ended, Warren announced, "Harper, I've been thinking that you should consider moving to Portland."

Harper barely stifled a gasp of surprise as she turned accusing eyes on Linc.

He put up both hands. "I swear. I didn't say a word."

Warren shrugged. "He didn't. Shelby and I aren't blind, though. It's obvious there's something special going on between you two. You should know that we thoroughly approve."

Harper wasn't sure what to say to that. Warren Stryker had no filter, apparently. He just came right out with whatever was on his mind. It was reassuring, though, to know Linc's dad saw her as a good match for his son—especially after the scathing disapproval she'd picked up from Linc's mom. "Well, thank you. And I am thinking of moving—but to Seattle, as a matter of fact."

To which Linc just had to add, "Don't worry, Dad. I'm not giving up. Somehow, I'll get her to change her plans…"

* * *

Shelby and Warren said good-night at a little after ten.

Harper intended to go on home then. But Linc whispered, "Stay. Just for a little while…"

She let him lead her upstairs.

"Your dad is so outspoken," she said an hour later, when they were cuddling in bed. "It's like, whatever he's thinking comes right out his mouth."

Linc traced slow circles on the bare skin of her shoulder. "Yeah. He's nothing like the father I grew up with. He used to be so preoccupied, so guarded and hard to talk to. He wasn't a good guy. But what can I say? I guess people really can change. I keep hoping my mom will get the memo on that."

She gazed up at him, meeting his eyes steadily. "She truly does not like me."

"She just has an agenda."

"Right. Getting you and Imogen back together…"

"That's never going to happen—and as for my mom, that she failed to get to know you is her loss." He tipped up her chin for a kiss.

She closed her eyes and thought how she really ought to get up and go home. But the bed was so comfy and Linc held her so tenderly. She turned on her side. He wrapped his body around her.

When she opened her eyes again, it was one in the morning. She popped to a sitting position and shoved her hair out of her eyes. "I gotta go."

But he pulled her back down. "Stay with me..." His voice coaxed and soothed her.

And she just didn't have the will to tell him no. His arms felt so good holding her close, and outside it was cold and drizzly and dark. He settled the covers back over them.

Nights like this, all wrapped up in his arms, she couldn't help thinking how fast the Christmas season was flying by. In a little more than a week, he and the kids would return to Portland.

It felt much too soon—to lose him. To lose *them*.

But she wouldn't be losing them, she reminded herself.

They'd agreed to keep seeing each other, to find ways to get together. He really did want to be with her.

And oh, she did love being with him.

When daylight came, Linc took the kids downstairs first, so that Harper could avoid having to answer Jayden's likely questions about why she'd been sleeping in Uncle Linc's room. She washed her face and combed her hair and put on yesterday's clothes.

When she entered the kitchen, everybody seemed happy to see her and no one asked where she'd spent the night. Really, it didn't feel awkward to her at all. She pitched right in helping Linc make breakfast for everyone.

Shelby and Warren stayed for lunch.

Finally, after hugs all around, good wishes for

the best Christmas ever and promises that they would get together again soon, Warren and his wife climbed into their rented Escalade and headed for Valentine Bay Executive Airport.

Back inside, Jayden went to his room to play with his train set and Maya fell asleep in her favorite spot on the floor by the tree. Harper stood over her, thinking that there was nothing so sweet as Maya, hugging her favorite stuffie, wearing a green velour top and matching leggings, a baby elf snoozing beneath the Christmas tree.

Strong arms came around her waist. Linc's warm breath brushed her cheek and his deep voice teased in her ear, "I like that you stayed with me last night."

She chuckled, but quietly, in order not to wake the sleeping elf at their feet. "You caught me at a weak moment."

"Good." He bit her earlobe. A shower of sparks danced across her skin. "I want you to go to your cottage and get your stuff."

"What stuff?"

"Clothes, fuzzy slippers, a toothbrush—whatever you need to sleep here with me from now on."

She loved that idea. Loved it too much. "You'll be gone back to Portland before you know it."

He nibbled on her neck. "All the more reason you should be in my bed every night while you can. I need my Harper fix. It's going to be hard enough going days on end without you if I can't convince you to change your mind and move to Portland—

but we're not there yet. I'm keeping a positive attitude about you and me and the amazing future we're going to build together. And the thing I want most—what you can give me for Christmas—is you in my bed every night, all night. At least until New Year's."

"I shouldn't…"

A low chuckle rumbled up. "That's a yes just waiting to be born. I know it is."

She turned in his arms and put her hands on his warm, broad chest. Beneath her palms, she could feel the steady beating of his heart. "All right, I'll bring a few things over. Now, let me go before Jayden wanders in and catches us canoodling."

Christmas Eve morning Jayden finally got his wish.

Linc was sound asleep when the boy bellowed, "We got snow!" from the other side of the master bedroom door.

The noise woke Maya, who let out a cry of surprise that echoed over the baby monitor by Linc's bed.

"What the…?" Linc startled awake as Harper's eyes popped open, too. They blinked at each other.

"Uncle Linc, you have to see!"

"Unc Winc! Up!" Maya chimed in.

Harper grinned sleepily at him. "You go. I'll be down in a minute." She looked so good, all rumpled and sleepy, her eyes low and lazy.

"I want to wake up next to you like this every morning."

"Uncle Linc, hurry up!"

She gave him a playful shove. "Go."

He rolled out of bed, put on some clothes and slipped out the door, where Jayden could barely contain his excitement.

"Let's go." The boy grabbed his hand.

"Whoa, hold on. We need to get your sister first."

"Hurry, then." Jayden turned for Maya's room, pulling Linc along behind him.

Linc got Maya up, changed her wet diaper and carried her downstairs, Jayden leading the way to the front door, which he unlocked and threw open.

"Snow!" With another shout of sheer joy, Jayden ran down the front steps in his slippers. Halfway along the front walk, he stopped and tipped his head up to the gray sky, opening his mouth wide, trying to catch snowflakes on his tongue.

"I got one!" he crowed. "It melts so fast!"

"Me, Unc Winc!" demanded Maya, bouncing up and down in his arms. "Me, too!"

So he carried her out beneath the sky. She tipped her head back and opened her mouth just like her brother was doing.

"We need to make a snowman," Jayden announced as they went back up the steps.

Linc herded him in through the door. "Let's have breakfast first and see if any of it sticks…"

In the kitchen, Harper was getting the coffee going. The kids didn't even blink at the sight of her. She'd become such a part of their lives in the past month, they never asked how she magically appeared in the kitchen when they came in from the cold.

Harper was having the best Christmas Eve ever.

Outside, the snow kept falling. By ten, there was enough to make a snowman, though a slightly malnourished-looking one. The snow was slowing by then, but the temperature stayed below freezing. Jayden's skinny snowman would no doubt last until Christmas Day.

At eleven, the kids and Linc Skyped with Jean and Alan, who were cruising the islands of French Polynesia. Linc called her over to join the conversation. Harper liked the grands a lot. They were good people.

For the rest of the day, they hung out, just the four of them. They played games, read stories and watched a couple of Disney movies.

Before the kids went to bed, they put out cookies and milk on the coffee table, in case Santa might want a snack.

It felt so right, just being here at the Stryker cottage with Linc and the kids. Like they really were building a family, the four of them. Together.

Was she getting a little carried away, spending too much time with them—with *him*? Losing sight of reality just a little bit?

So what? Why should she go home to her quiet, empty cottage when everything she wanted was right here? Yeah, reality mattered. But why shouldn't she let go and enjoy every moment of this perfect holiday season?

She understood the facts. The New Year would come. He would go back to Portland to live in a house that looked like something from *Architectural Digest* and run an international shipping company. She would head north on a wing and prayer.

And really, so what? It was still December. Her uncertain future remained out there, waiting for her. She didn't have to rush to meet it.

Why not lighten up a little, go with the flow? At the least, she would have a beautiful Christmas with a wonderful man.

And just maybe, it would all work out and they would end up together. Stranger things had happened.

Why shouldn't she *believe* that she was meant to be with Linc and the kids? It was the season of miracles, after all. And maybe this particular miracle— of her and this amazing guy and these two beautiful children—maybe it wasn't so crazy to reach out and claim what Linc offered her. Maybe he was tailor-made for her.

Why couldn't he be right about the two of them? Why shouldn't they be together?

Why not go ahead and make the move to Portland? The job prospects weren't quite as good for her there, but Portland State offered an accredited master's program in architecture, too. Jobwise, something was bound to come up.

Plus, it would be less expensive to get a place in Portland.

And most important, she wouldn't have to leave her love…

Love?

Wait. No.

She shouldn't let herself do that. It was too soon. She couldn't afford to go to the love place.

Slowly, she drew a deep breath and waited for the denials to rush in. Because she wasn't ready for love. Not now. Not for a few years yet, anyway. She needed to find her way as an adult first, get her own place in the right city and start creating a whole new career before she let herself get wrapped up in a man.

No. Uh-uh. Not ready for love.

Too bad love had found her, anyway.

She sat on the sofa by the fire in the living room, with the tree blazing bright and the outdoor lights winking merrily at her through the picture window. The kids were in bed. Linc had gone to the kitchen to open a bottle of Christmas Eve bubbly.

And here she sat on the sofa, unable to deny her true feelings anymore.

Love.

Love had happened to her.

She'd taken a temporary job to build up her bank account and ended up falling in love with the boss—only, no.

Not the boss.

She was her own boss, an independent contractor, as she'd made so painfully clear to Linc right from the beginning.

So, then. Boss or not, she loved him. Was *in* love with him.

Lincoln Stryker is my love.

It sounded so good inside her head.

But yeah, it was probably way too early to tell him how she felt. So she wouldn't. Not yet. They would discuss the future again at some point before he went back to Portland. And when they did, she would tell him that yes, she wanted to be near him and the kids. She would agree that yes, she would come to Portland in February and start looking for work.

"You look happy." Linc sat down beside her, an open bottle of champagne in one hand, two flutes in the other.

"I *am* happy. It's been a great day. The best kind of Christmas Eve, quiet and cozy with at least a token amount of snow."

He filled the two glasses, handed one to her and offered a toast. "To skinny snowmen and Disney movies."

"I will definitely drink to that." She tapped her glass to his, enjoyed a fizzy sip and wondered how she'd lived all her life up till now without him in it.

"I have something for you…" He set down his glass and went to the tree. Crouching, he pulled a mug-sized box from among the many brightly wrapped packages.

She grinned. She had a travel mug for him, too—and a pair of snowman socks. But she'd been assuming they would wait until Christmas morning to do the gift thing.

He took his place beside her again. "Merry Christmas."

"I should open it now?"

He nodded. "Please."

She untied the bow, tore open the pretty paper and took the lid off the box. Within, a smaller box, also brightly wrapped, sat in a cocoon of red tissue paper.

Something happened in her chest, something warm as a toasty fire, bubbly and bright as champagne.

Because that smaller box?

It was a ring-sized box.

She blinked at it in its cradle of bright tissue and that warm, fizzy feeling in her chest was expanding, taking over her whole body.

Really, she shouldn't be reacting like this—like he'd just handed her the moon all wrapped in Christmas paper. It was too early.

Too soon, and she knew it. They couldn't go rushing into something so huge as what could be waiting in this ring-sized box.

She put her hand to her chest where her heart pounded like it wanted to get out and bounce around the room for joy. This couldn't be right.

The words of love had yet to be spoken. They'd met barely a month ago.

No doubt about it. It was much too soon.

And yet, well, if it was too soon, why did it *feel* so right?

Breathless, yearning, ready to take the most impossible leap, she lifted the smaller box free of the tissue. Carefully, fingers moving slow and dreamlike, she set the other box on the coffee table and unwrapped the little one.

The box inside was black velvet. A ring box, no question about it.

Could this really be happening?

Stunned at her own reaction of sheer, unbounded happiness, she went with it. It was not what she'd planned, so far from anything she'd expected—of herself, or of him.

And yet…

She *was* in love with Linc. And it didn't matter that it had happened fast.

It was the real thing.

And damn it, she couldn't wait to say yes.

Because really? It was perfect—*they* were perfect, her and Linc, together.

They were right for each other and she loved the kids and she'd already decided she would move to Portland instead of Seattle. Who had she been kidding, telling herself that she didn't want more from him?

She *did* want more. She wanted everything, a forever, together, with Linc and the kids.

"Well? Are you going to open it?" He leaned closer, his voice low, kind of teasing.

As she raised the tiny hinged lid, her hands weren't shaking hardly at all.

Inside, a gorgeous pair of diamond earrings twinkled up at her.

She gaped down at them. Her lips felt numb and her heart had paused midbeat.

What had just happened?

What was the matter with her?

All her talk about not getting in too deep, taking it slow—and she'd just lost her mind assuming Linc suddenly wanted to marry her.

She needed to get a grip and get it fast.

Linc asked, sounding hopeful, "Do you like them?"

They were quite beautiful, two gorgeous round stones. And there was no way she could accept them.

She forced her head up and made herself meet his eyes.

Linc's brow furrowed in concern—because apparently, she had no control over her expression. "What is it? Harper, what's wrong?"

She pushed out appreciative words. "They're gorgeous."

The space between his eyebrows smoothed out. "Whew. For a minute there, I thought you hated them."

"Linc, I..."

Twin lines drew down between his eyebrows. "Okay, you'd better tell me what I did wrong."

Her silly heart had started in again—too fast and too hard. It was knocking away, a wrecking ball inside her chest. Her cheeks burned with heat. She wasn't ready yet, to love like this.

She had stuff to do, things to figure out. She couldn't go giving her heart over to a rich guy from Portland. "Linc, I got you an insulated travel mug and some snowman socks."

He sat back an inch. He had that look, the one a guy gets when he knows that whatever he says next will not be the right thing. "Great. I need a new mug and fun socks work for me."

Crap. No wonder she was in love with him. He might be hot and rich with the world at his feet, but he was also a good guy. "We've known each other for a month. It's too soon for diamonds, you know?"

"No, it's not. Not if you like them. It doesn't have to be a big deal. I bought them for you because I think they'll look great on you. Come on, I want you to have them."

"Well, thank you. But no. I really can't take them." She grabbed his hand, turned it over, set the velvet box in his palm and folded his fingers over it.

And right now, well, she just couldn't stay here. She needed to get back to her own place. She needed distance, to be away from him.

Her heart ached so bad. She felt like a fool—which was in no way his fault.

She didn't want to worry him. But really, she had to go home.

She said, "Linc, listen…"

He dropped the velvet box on the coffee table and took both her hands, his eyes probing, insistent. "Talk to me. Tell me. What's going on with you? What went wrong?"

"I just need to go home, okay?"

"No. It's not okay. I want to know what's going on."

"Please." She eased her fingers from his grip. He let go reluctantly. "I just need a little time to myself. I need to go home for the night. Really. Think about it. I've been spending every moment here."

"And I love that. I want you here with me—come on, just tell me what's wrong."

She stood. "I'm going to go. I'll be here tomorrow morning. I'll do breakfast—blueberry pancakes, just like we planned." She backed away as she spoke. "We'll open the presents, go up to Daniel's for Christmas dinner. It'll be great."

"Harper." His wonderful face—the face she loved, God help her—showed utter confusion. "Please."

She swallowed hard and shook her head, "I just need to go home. Everything's fine, really."

"No, it's not. Talk to me. Tell me what's wrong."

"I, um… What can I say? See you tomorrow." And then she whirled on her heel and got out of there.

Chapter Twelve

Linc longed to bolt to his feet and run after her. But she'd made it unnervingly clear she was leaving and nothing short of physical restraint would keep her there.

The sound of the front door closing behind her made him want to grab the champagne and throw it through the picture window—or maybe at the tree.

He lifted both hands and raked them back through his hair.

Really, what just happened? Yeah, he got that he'd screwed up somehow. But why couldn't she have just told him what he'd done wrong so he could fix it?

It wasn't like her to jump up and run away like that. She'd seemed so happy, that beautiful face all aglow—and then she saw the earrings—and shut down.

It had to be the earrings. Maybe she had a thing against diamonds.

But why?

Uh-uh.

It just made no damn sense.

He sat there in the living room for an hour or so, drinking the excellent champagne and hardly tasting it, resisting the urge to text her, to try to coax her into giving him just a hint of what had gone wrong with her.

But he didn't get out his phone. If she were willing to talk to him, she would have done it before she ran out.

Eventually, he got up and dealt with the cookies and milk the kids had left out for Santa. He turned out the lights and climbed the stairs to his bedroom alone. He still had no idea what had gone wrong with Harper.

He just knew that somehow, he needed to fix it.

At her cottage, Harper put on her oldest, softest flannel pajamas and then paced the floor.

She felt like such a loser. Poor Linc. She'd left him sitting there wondering what was the matter with her. He had no idea that he'd broken her heart—scratch that.

Linc had *not* broken her heart. It was not his fault that she'd gotten carried away with this thing between them, let her emotions take over when the plan was to keep it fun and no-pressure, to move their relationship along at a nice, reasonable pace.

That she'd come unglued was *her* fault. She needed to deal with that and then apologize to him for running out on him tonight.

And it would all work out, she reminded herself. She'd known going in that this thing with him was temporary. She'd had her eyes wide-open—and then, bam! Love had hit her like a safe dropped on her head.

But so what?

Nothing bad had happened, really—well, except for her bizarre behavior at the sight of those earrings. Linc had already made it clear he wanted to keep seeing her. Unless she'd scared him away with her disappearing act tonight, they would still end up talking about the future, about finding ways to spend more time together.

It was fine. Good. In the morning, she would downplay what had happened tonight. And later, Christmas night, when the kids were in bed and they were finally alone, she would apologize for her out-there behavior and say she hoped that they could let it go and move on.

The smell of coffee and breakfast scented the air as Linc brought the kids downstairs the next morning.

Harper was already there, looking a little tired,

maybe, but heart-stoppingly beautiful in a red sweater and white jeans that clung to every perfect curve, her waterfall of golden hair in loose waves down her back.

All morning, as they ate the breakfast she'd prepared and then opened the mountain of presents beneath the tree, she was sweet and bubbly, brimming with holiday cheer.

She really did seem okay—a little too cheerful, maybe. But overall, fine.

Which had him feeling more bewildered than ever.

Could he have read last night all wrong?

No.

She'd jumped to her feet out of nowhere and announced she had to go. And then she'd run away from him, out the door.

No matter how wide her brilliant smile this morning, she was not okay.

At eleven, they bundled up in coats, hats and winter gloves. Outside, it was raining, and Jayden's skinny snowman was no more. With four wonderful-smelling pies that Harper had baked and some presents for the Bravo kids, they piled into the Rover to head up to Daniel's.

Jayden and Maya were excited. Harper was all smiles.

As for Linc, he was no closer to figuring out what was going on with her than he'd been when she walked out on him the night before.

* * *

"What's going on?" demanded Hailey. She'd been lying in wait in the upstairs hall at Daniel's when Harper put a cranky Maya down for a nap in one of the empty bedrooms. "We need to talk."

Harper took her sister by the shoulders and looked her squarely in the eye. "There's nothing."

Hailey scowled at her. "You know I hate it when you lie to me. You've been weird all day. Too smiley. *Fake* smiley."

Harper groaned and pulled her sister close. "Can't talk about it now," she whispered.

Hailey hugged her. "When?"

"I'll call you. I promise. Just please, let's *not*. Not today. I'm not ready to go there." *And maybe I never will be.*

"When?" Hailey demanded in her usual take-charge way. "Did Linc—"

"Linc did nothing wrong."

"But he *is* the problem, right?"

Laughing a little, Harper pulled back. "Later. We'll talk. I promise."

Hailey wasn't happy, but at least she let it go for now. They went back downstairs with their arms around each other and joined Linc and Roman, who were talking real estate in the family room.

It was after eight when they got back in the Range Rover to return to the cottage. Yesterday's snow was long gone. A drizzly rain was falling. Exhausted from a day full of presents, good food and fun, both kids snoozed in the back seat. Even Jayden was too tired to talk.

"It was a great day," Linc said quietly, his face illuminated by the dashboard lights.

"Yeah." Harper sent him what she hoped was a genuine-looking smile. Inside, her every nerve hummed, and her stomach had managed to tie itself in a tight chain of knots. Once the kids were in bed, she would have to clear the air with him. Too bad she'd yet to figure out what she would say to him, how to apologize for her strange behavior without saying too much.

One month, she reminded herself. That's how long they'd known each other. Too soon for the big talk about love and forever, that much was certain.

Maybe she could just grab him and kiss him and let nature do the job for her. They would go upstairs to his big bed and she would exhaust him with sex. By the time she'd finished with him, he wouldn't remember his name—let alone her flaky behavior the night before.

It would be fine. She would keep it light. They would have a sexy Christmas night together. And she wouldn't have to admit that she'd fallen hopelessly in love with him and didn't know what to do with the strength of her own emotions.

They rode down the hill and across town to the cottage without saying much. But it didn't seem *too* tense to her.

At least, not until they rounded that last turn in the twisting driveway up to the cottage to find a silver Jaguar parked in front of the house and three women perched on the front step—his mother, a beautiful brunette who had to be Imogen. And another woman the same age as Alicia, who looked a lot like the glamorous brunette.

Linc could not believe what his eyes were seeing.

His mother and Sarah wore cool, determined expressions.

As for Imogen, she was dressed all in white, including her high-heeled boots and the fur collar of her big coat. Her lips were bright red and stretched in a defiant smile.

He pulled the Rover to a stop and she rose to her feet.

"Just give me a minute," he whispered to Harper, trying not to wake the children sleeping in the back seat.

"What's going on, Linc?"

"I have no idea."

He shoved open the driver's door and got out, taking care to shut it quietly behind him. By then, Sarah and his mother had risen to their feet. As for Imogen, she was already on him.

"Darling. Merry Christmas. It's so good to see you." She threw her arms around him and shoved her face up for a kiss.

He managed to pull back before her red lips

touched his. Taking her by the arms, he held her away and exerted superhuman effort not to go off on her right then and there. "What are you doing here?"

She tipped her head to the side and faked a wounded look. Her eyes told the truth, though. They glittered with reckless fire. "Oh, Linc. You know why I'm here. You wouldn't talk to me. I couldn't stand it anymore. I had to see you, *be* with you, find a way to make everything right between us."

It was a nightmare—his mother and Sarah, self-righteous and ramrod straight, glaring at him from the porch. Harper in the Rover, witnessing this awfulness. Imogen gazing up at him, uttering desperate words as her eyes threatened dire consequences if he failed to give her what she wanted.

Had she always been like this?

He knew the answer. She had, and he'd gone along with it, telling himself that they understood each other, that she was charming when she wanted to be, that he was ready to get married and the two of them were a good fit.

Fit.

As though a wife were a shirt or a new suit. She only had to be well-made, of quality material…

He gazed into those furiously glittering eyes and wondered. At himself. At her. At his mother's ongoing, vindictive bitterness. Was there any way to get through to either of them?

"I just need to talk to you," she pleaded. "I want some time with you, alone."

"And so you came on Christmas night and brought both our mothers?"

"Yes." She tossed her tumbling, dark curls. "I couldn't wait a moment longer. And our moms are here to provide the moral support I so desperately need."

"This is completely unacceptable. It really does have to stop."

In the Range Rover, Harper couldn't take it anymore. Clearly, Linc and the gorgeous brunette who gazed up at him so desperately had more to work out.

And Harper had no place here. Time to go home.

Quietly, hoping the kids would sleep through whatever was about to happen next, she pushed open her door, stepped out and shut it behind her. "Linc, I'm going to go."

All eyes swung her way.

"This must be the nanny?" said Imogen, nodding, her ferocious smile growing wider, perfect white teeth flashing with malice. "Yes, you are so right. It's time for you to go."

"Shut up, Imogen." Linc tossed the words over his shoulder, and then gentled his voice. "It's okay, Harper. Just get back in the Rover."

"No, Linc. I'm not going to do that."

From behind him on the porch, Alicia called, "Let her go, Linc. She has no business here. This is a family matter."

He turned to his mother. "Don't," he said low. "Just don't."

Meanwhile, Imogen lifted her left hand and waved Harper goodbye. A giant engagement diamond sparkled on her ring finger.

Somehow, the woman still had Linc's ring.

And it hurt. It hurt bad, that he'd given this woman his ring, that she'd been his fiancée a short time ago. Seeing that ring was a blow straight to the heart.

Because Harper loved him. She loved him so much. How could this have happened to her in a few too-short weeks? She was in so far over her head, drowning, going down for the final time, staring up at the sky far above, knowing she was done for.

She turned her gaze on Linc. "While you're carrying on out here, please don't forget that there are two little children asleep in that car."

"Of course not. Harper, don't go…" He looked at her as though she was everything to him.

Yet his gift to her had been earrings. The woman behind him, backed up by her mother and his mother, too—that woman got the ring.

"You have people you need to deal with here." And right now, Harper knew she was only in the way. "Good night, Linc." She started walking.

Silence followed her. She walked faster, never once looking back.

Chapter Thirteen

Linc watched her go, longing only to follow, to convince her to stop, to wait—to turn around.

But why *should* she be here? This wasn't her fight. It was his damn mess and he needed to clean it the hell up.

First things first.

He turned to address all three angry women, modulating his voice to a low, controlled rumble. "There are two innocent children in the back seat of my car. As long as they're nearby, I don't want one thoughtless or mean word from any of you. Is that clear?"

All three of them muttered, "Of course," simultaneously.

"Terrific. I'm going to get them both out of their car seats now and herd them inside. Just make yourselves comfortable. Help yourselves to a stiff drink, why don't you? Keep your thoughts to yourselves until I've safely tucked Jayden and Maya in bed."

"All right," said Imogen.

"We will," said his mother.

The kids really were worn out.

When he took Maya from her car seat, she wrapped her little arms around his neck and went right back to sleep. Jayden took his hand and walked along beside him, murmuring softly, "Hi, Grandma," as he went up the steps.

"Merry Christmas, Jayden," Alicia said softly.

Not trusting her in the least, Linc sent her a warning frown. She stared right back at him, but kept her mouth shut.

He left the door open for her and the Whitmans. Holding firmly to Jayden's hand, cradling Maya close, he headed straight for the stairs.

Twenty minutes later, he came back down. The women sat in the living room. His mother had opened a bottle of white wine. They each had a glass.

He stood by the tree and addressed all three of them. "What do you want?" It was probably a mistake to ask that question, but he really did need the answer. The sooner he could find out what they wanted, the sooner he could deal with them and they could go away.

Alicia said, "You owe it to your fiancée to hear what she has to say."

"She is not my fiancée and I owe her nothing." He went right on before anyone could argue. "But all right. Imogen and I will speak privately, after which all three of you will leave."

The women just sat there for several seconds as he wondered what they'd thought could possibly be gained by ambushing him at the cottage on Christmas night.

Finally, Imogen replied in a wounded tone, "Oh, Linc, yes. To talk to you, to get it all out and make myself finally clear to you. That's all I've ever wanted…"

"Great, then. This should be brief. Let's go into my office."

It was not brief.

For the next two hours, behind the shut door of his office, Imogen alternately cried and ranted, pleaded and accused. He sat in a club chair across from her and tried to listen without judgment or anger.

He didn't succeed, but he did manage to be outwardly gentle and firm, patient and kind—and not to say anything he would end up regretting. There really was nothing more for him to say to her, and he was just waiting for her to realize that she had nothing to say that mattered to him.

She cried all the harder. He handed her some tissues and waited some more.

"I'll never get through to you, will I?" She sniffled and dabbed at her eyes.

He answered in a mild tone. "I don't love you, Imogen. We're through. There's nothing more we need to say."

At that, she burst into tears again, tore off the engagement ring she shouldn't even be wearing and threw it at him.

He caught it in midflight, got up and locked it in a drawer of his desk. Was that an insulting thing to do? Maybe. But he didn't want her grabbing it back and waving it around as though it proved that they were still together.

"You have no heart!" she cried. "I suppose this is it, then. I'll go and you'll be calling the nanny to warm up your bed."

It was a bad moment. He almost lost it. He wanted to shout that he loved Harper Bravo, that she'd brought joy and laughter, tenderness and hope into his life and the lives of his niece and nephew.

But that wouldn't be right. He needed to say the words to Harper first, before he spoke them to anyone else. And the last thing he should ever do was to shout them in anger at his ex. "You don't know what you're talking about and I'll thank you to leave Harper out of this."

There were more accusations. He did his best to tune them out.

Finally, Imogen jumped to her feet. "That's it. That's all. I quit. I am finished with you, Lincoln Stryker."

"All right, then. We understand each other at last. Time for you to go."

Ten minutes later, he stood on the front step and watched the Jaguar drive away. His mother had gone with them. He didn't know what to do about her, and he kind of wondered if he ever would.

Inside, he poured out the last of the wine and put the empty bottle in the recycle bin. He loaded the glasses into the dishwasher, longing the whole time to call Harper, to make sure she was all right. But it was after eleven and he had a bad feeling she wouldn't welcome his call.

Upstairs in his room, he settled on sending her a text.

They're finally gone and not coming back. I miss you. When you get this, would you just let me know that you're okay?

He hit Send and then stared at the screen for a while, willing her to reply. She didn't.

So he got ready for bed, climbed between the covers alone and turned off the light.

He was lying on his back, staring blindly into the darkness, longing for the feel of her, the scent of her, there, close to him—when his phone lit up on the nightstand.

Grabbing it, he read:

I'm all right. And I've got some things I really need to do at the theater, stuff to catch up on. I haven't had a day off in a while. Tell the kids I'll be back soon.

"Not a chance," he growled at the dark room and the bright screen. "I need you here..."

But the dark room wasn't listening, and the bright screen had dimmed.

He ground his teeth together, hating that he had no choice but to give her the time she wanted.

Plus, she was right, damn it. Tonight had been a horror show. The least he could do was not argue if she needed some space.

Of course. When will I see you, then?

I would like two days off.

Hell, no. He needed to see her, to touch her, to find a way to reassure her that everything would work out.

All right. Get some rest. See you soon.

And by the way, I love you.

Good night, Linc.

Good night.

Two days, he thought as he set the phone aside. *In two days, she'll be back, and I'll make it up to her.* In two days, he would tell her that he loved her, that what he wanted more than anything was the chance to spend the rest of his life with her...

Harper had lied. There was nothing she just *had* to do at the theater. In fact, on the day after Christmas, she didn't leave the cottage. She dragged around in her pajamas, devouring a whole bag of Cheetos and half a carton of Tillamook Mudslide.

Being in love was awful, she decided. It was painful and messy, and she wanted nothing to do with it.

But she missed Linc so much. She had this enormous emptiness inside her, and the only thing that would fill it was his touch on her skin, his voice in her ear, his lips pressed to hers.

Three times that day, she almost threw a coat over her pj's and marched to the other cottage to declare her undying love.

Somehow, she stopped herself.

That evening, Hailey texted her.

I have a bad feeling. Are you all right?

She wrote back that she was fine.
Hailey replied:

Why am I not reassured? We need to talk.

Can't right now. Busy.

Doing what, exactly?

Things. Lots of things…

When, then?

Soon.

You can't put me off forever, Harp.

I love you, Lee-Lee. TTYS.

Early the next morning, on her second day off from dealing with Linc, Harper received a text from Mia Acevedo.

Got a minute? Can we talk?

Harper hit the phone icon. "Happy almost New Year. What's up?"

"Sam and I have been talking. Business is really taking off. We need another designer and we need it to be you."

Harper's pulse went haywire. She made herself draw a slow, deep breath. "Is this a job offer?"

"Yes, it is. Can you move to Portland? We would love it if you could start, say, January 15?"

Her heart ached as it soared. She had no idea how

things were going to work out with Linc. If they were over, she would rather be miles from him in Seattle—or better yet, Tanzania, or maybe Timbuktu.

But she wanted to work with Mia. The offer was a dream come true. And even if she and Linc weren't destined to be a couple, there was room enough in Rose City for both of them.

Mia quoted a salary that Harper could actually live on—frugally, in a studio apartment. Which sounded pretty much perfect to her.

Harper said yes and promised to drive down the week after New Year's. She would find herself a place to live, meet with Mia to fill out forms and discuss all the aspects of her new job with Acevedo Hybrid Homes.

When she hung up, she did a happy dance around the kitchen—after which she dropped into a chair at the table and burst into tears. She had the perfect starting job in her new career.

And she had no idea what was going to happen with Linc. She missed Maya and Jayden, yet here she sat in her pajamas for the second day, alone in the cottage that had seemed way too big and empty ever since Hailey had moved out.

She heard a car drive up outside and knew who it was without having to look. Sometimes it was like that between her and Hailey. One of them would think of the other.

And the other would appear.

Her sister came in through the short hall from the front door. "What's going on here?" Hailey shrugged out of her coat, draped it on a chair and went straight to Harper. "Why are you crying?" She grabbed Harper's hand and hauled her up into her arms.

Harper hugged her tight. "Now you've done it, got me sobbing again…"

"Again?"

"Shut up and hug me."

Hailey did hug her. She held Harper close and made soothing noises until the crying stopped. "Better?"

"Mmm-hmm, a little."

"All right, then." Hailey guided Harper back into her chair, handed her a box of tissues, poured them each a cup of coffee and demanded, "Tell me exactly what happened."

Harper let it all out—from her new job that would mean she would be living in Portland, to the awfulness of what had occurred Christmas night and even her self-defense strategy of avoiding Linc since then.

Hailey congratulated her on the new job—and then peered at her more closely. "You just said Linc texted you after the evil ex and the two mothers from hell finally left, that he asked you to come back. I don't get why you're crying. It's so obvious the man's in love with you."

Harper just sniffled, waved a dismissing hand and shook her head.

But Hailey was Hailey. She ran the show. And that meant she kept the pressure on until Harper told the rest of it—about the "ring" that had turned out to be earrings. "And then, well, his ex showed up wearing the giant diamond he'd bought her."

"But they *are* broken up, right?"

"Yes. They are."

"It's not his fault that his ex kept the ring and had the bad taste and terrible judgment to keep wearing it."

"I know that. Of course, I do. But, Lee-Lee, he gave *her* a ring. It just hurt, that's all. That *I* got the earrings and *she* got engaged to him."

Hailey scooted up close and enfolded Harper in another much-needed hug. "Honey, men mess up. The good ones finally get it right. Linc Stryker is one of the good ones. You need *not* to let that man get away."

She leaned her head on Hailey's shoulder. "Easy for you to say."

"Hey. Uh-uh." Hailey put a finger under Harper's chin. "Let me see those eyes."

"Fine." Harper glared at her.

"Don't you see what's going on here?"

"Um, nope. Not really…"

"Harp, this is *your* love story. You've got to own it. You've spent all your life behind the scenes, making the magic happen for the ones who take center stage. Now it's *your* turn. This is when you need to be the center of attention. You can't hide your light."

"Ugh. You and your theater metaphors. I can't even."

Tenderly, Hailey guided a straggling curl behind Harper's ear. "Sweetheart. Do you love him?"

She hard-swallowed and told the scary truth. "Yes. I do."

"Then you need to step up and tell him so."

Linc sat on the living room floor carefully combing the shiny brunette locks of Maya's new Carla Marie doll. "How's that?"

"O-*kay*!" Maya took the doll and began removing her dress. She was in love with Carla Marie's new clothes, the ones Harper had made and given Maya for Christmas. Maya was constantly changing the doll's outfits—meaning Linc had to do the buttoning and snapping that Maya's chubby fingers couldn't quite handle yet.

Harper...

Just thinking her name made him long to go find her. He hadn't seen her since Christmas night and she wasn't due back until tomorrow afternoon.

The waiting was killing him. He wondered constantly how she was doing, had to keep resisting the urge to call her—or better yet, march over to her cottage and beg her to talk to him, tell him everything that was bothering her, find a way to convince her that all he wanted was her. He kept going over what he needed to say to her, kept rehearsing how he might manage to tell her he loved her, *would* love her, forever, without scaring her away.

The doorbell rang. Maya's curly head shot up from trying to pull purple leggings onto Carla Marie's chunky bare legs. "Hawp?" She dropped the doll. Levering forward, hands flat on the floor, she stuck her butt in the air. From that position, she popped up-right. "Hawp!" And off she went, headed for the door.

Jayden came pounding down the stairs. "Who's at the door?"

Linc ordered his racing heart to settle down as he stood. "Let's go find out."

It wasn't Harper, but the kids were glad, anyway, because it was Hailey. They loved Hailey almost as much as they loved her sister.

"Lee-Lee!" crowed Maya and lifted her arms. "Up."

"Hailey," said Jayden. "Come in. I need to show you my train station."

"Hey, guys." Hailey swung Maya up in her arms.

Linc stepped back so Harper's sister could enter. "Good to see you."

Jayden tugged on the hem of her jacket. "Come on, Hailey. My train set is upstairs, and I got a second depot for Christmas."

She grinned down at him. "Hold on a minute, big guy." And she looked up at Linc. "I was just at the other cottage…"

His pulse rocketed into the stratosphere. "Is she all right?"

"As a matter of fact, it occurred to me that you could use a sitter for an hour or two. You can go check on her, maybe tell her all the things you probably should have said before she came face-to-face with your ex, who for some unknown reason was still wearing your ring…" He winced at the memory as Hailey continued, "And while we're on the subject of diamonds, I would also advise that you never give a woman you're serious about a small velvet jewelry box—that is, unless it contains an engagement ring."

It all came way too clear—Imogen wearing his ring, the earrings he'd tried to give Harper. "She thought I was proposing, that the earring box had a ring in it—and then she saw the ring I gave Imogen…"

Hailey regarded him patiently—and the kids stared, too. "How do you think that made my sister feel?"

"Okay, yeah. It all makes an awful kind of sense now…"

"I'm so pleased you get that."

"I need to talk to her."

"Yes, you do."

Linc grabbed his jacket off the hook by the door. "I'll, um, be back soon…"

"Take your time," Hailey advised. "We're fine, aren't we, guys?"

"Yes!" declared Jayden. "We got stuff to do."

"We fine!" Maya agreed.

Linc stared at Hailey, hardly daring to believe that Harper might just be waiting at home for him to come and get her.

"Why are you still here?" Hailey waved him off with an impatient flick of her free hand. *"Go."*

After Hailey left the cottage, Harper poured herself a third cup of coffee. She sat at the table, still in her red plaid flannel pajamas, thinking about washing her hair, putting her clothes on, working up the courage to go to Linc and tell him that she loved him.

Hailey said she needed to be the star of her own story. But she didn't *feel* like a star. She felt like an unprepared understudy with dirty hair.

And was that a theater metaphor?

Hailey would be so proud.

The doorbell chimed.

What now?

Reluctantly, she got up and went to the door, pulling it wide with no clue who would be waiting on the other side.

"Hey, beautiful," he said.

She blinked in disbelief that he was actually standing on her doorstep. "My hair's dirty and I'm still in my pajamas."

A smile quirked the corners of his wonderful mouth. "Like I said, you are absolutely beautiful. Can I come in?"

"Uh, yeah. Sure." She stepped back for him to enter and then closed the door behind him. "The kids?"

"Hailey's with them at the other cottage."

She groaned and felt the hot flush as it swept up her throat. "I should have known. How much did she tell you?"

He reached out, ran a slow, tender finger over the curve of her cheek. Her nerve endings sparked in sheer pleasure at the lingering touch. He said, "She just explained a few things I really needed to understand."

"Oh, God. She told you about Imogen's ring and the earrings, right?" She kind of wished the hardwood floor would just open up and swallow her whole.

But then he said, "I love you, Harper. You're my light in the darkness, my heart and my soul. I have no excuse for Imogen. I was a man without a clue. But I'm not that guy anymore. And I do want to marry you. Whenever you're ready—the sooner the better. I should have just made my move, but I really thought it was the right thing, not to push you too fast…"

She had no words. Center stage, in the spotlight. And she'd forgotten her lines. "Linc. Oh, Linc…" She reached for him.

"Harper. Damn it. At last." He grabbed her close and wrapped her up in those big, strong arms.

And then his mouth came down on hers. Heat and hope and love and longing pulsing through her, she jumped up and he caught her as she wrapped her legs around him, twined her whole body around him, like a vine.

"That way." She broke the kiss just long enough to point down the hall. He carried her where she pointed. When they reached her room, she grabbed the door frame before he could stride past it. "I love you, too. In here…"

He took her in there and laid her on her unmade bed. She pulled him down with her and started pushing on his jacket. "Get rid of this. Get rid of everything…"

They proceeded to tear frantically at each other's

clothes. It was awkward and ridiculous and absolutely smoking hot.

Finally, when both of them were stark naked, they rolled together on the bed, kissing endlessly, hands all over each other, unable to get close enough, unwilling to let go.

"Crap," he muttered. "No condoms…"

"No problem. Remember? I do get the shot—and I trust you, Linc. Completely." She hitched her legs around his lean waist, reached down between them and guided him home.

"I love you."

"I love you."

And then no more words were necessary. They were just Linc and Harper, joined in every way at last, making promises with their bodies, the most important promises, the kind two people in love are forever bound to keep.

Epilogue

Harper never leased that studio apartment. In the first week of January, she moved to the Forest Park house with Linc and the kids.

The new nanny, Elaine, started the first day Harper went to work for Mia and Sam. Elaine was kind and affectionate. Jayden and Maya adored her—but they came running when Harper got home.

It was during the third week in January that Linc took Harper shopping for the perfect ring. She chose a round, pale blue sapphire flanked by diamonds on a platinum band.

She and Linc got married in Valentine Bay on the last Saturday in March, a small celebration, mostly family. Maya was the flower girl and Jayden the ring bearer. Harper had Hailey for her maid of honor and Daniel to give her away. Linc's mother, now back in Italy, said she couldn't make it.

But Warren and Shelby came from Vail, with their beautiful new baby, Shaniece. And though Alan and Jean Hollister were still on their world cruise, they attended the ceremony via Skype.

When Harper threw the bouquet, she made sure that Hailey caught it. After all, Hailey and Roman were getting married at the end of May—and except for the long-lost Finn, Hailey would be the last of the Bravo siblings to say, "I do."

Up at Daniel's house after the wedding, Harper made a point to raise a glass of champagne to the parents they all missed to this day. "To Mom and Dad. We love you so much!"

Her words were picked up and echoed through the room.

Next, Harper saluted the brother they'd yet to find. "To Finn. Wherever you are, we *will* find you someday."

"To Finn," everyone answered in unison, each face solemn, the women with teary eyes, as they drank to the ongoing search for the brother they'd lost so long ago.

On the first Friday in May, Harper sat at her drafting table at Acevedo Hybrid Homes when her cell vibrated with a call from Hailey.

Harper picked up. "Hey. What's going on?"

"You will not believe this." Hailey spoke low—as if in awe or maybe shock.

"What? Tell me. You're freaking me out."

"It's official. We *didn't* find Finn."

"What are you talking about?"

"Finn has found *us*."

"Hailey, slow down. Finn *found* us?"

"That's right. A couple of hours ago, Finn—who lives in New York now and goes by Ian McNeill—walked into Valentine Logging and asked to speak with Daniel."

Harper's stomach hollowed out. If she hadn't already been sitting down, she just might have fallen flat on her ass. "You're messing with me."

"Never would I mess about Finn. He's coming up to Daniel's for dinner tonight. Can you get here?"

"Are you kidding me? I wouldn't miss it for the world. I'm calling Linc to see if he can come, too. But one way or another, you can count on me to be there."

When she hung up with Hailey, Harper just sat there for a minute, holding the phone, hardly daring to believe that their vanished brother had come home at last.

It felt so huge and impossible, the final closing of an open circle, her family reunited after so many years. She called Linc.

"How's my beautiful wife?"

"Stunned. Flabbergasted. Thunderstruck. And every other word that means shocked beyond belief. My brother Finn has come home. I need to go to Valentine Bay—now."

Her husband didn't hesitate. "I'll call Oxana to pack us a bag and tell Elaine to get the kids ready."

"Should I go get them?"

"No. You can leave your car there. I'll pick up the kids and swing by for you within the hour."

"Wait—what about Oscar?" Oscar was the rescue dog Jayden had chosen at the animal shelter two weeks before. They'd planned to adopt a puppy, but one look at the wiry-haired five-year-old mutt with the patch on one eye, and Jayden had changed his mind.

"How about we just bring him?" said Linc.

She laughed. "Sure. Bring Oscar. Why not? It's a family affair."

"Would you call the property manager to open up the cottage for us?"

"Will do."

"Sit tight, my love," he said softly. "We're on our way."

* * * * *

WE HOPE YOU ENJOYED
THIS BOOK FROM

HARLEQUIN
SPECIAL
EDITION

Believe in love. Overcome obstacles. Find happiness.

Relate to finding comfort and strength in the support of loved ones and enjoy the journey no matter what life throws your way.

6 NEW BOOKS AVAILABLE EVERY MONTH!

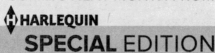

*When Grace Williams topples from the balcony at the
new Hotel Fortune, the last thing she expects is to find
love with her new bosses' brother. Wiley Fortune has
looks, money and charm to spare. But Grace's past
makes her wary of investing her heart. This time, she is
holding out for the real deal...*

Read on for a sneak peek at
Her Texas New Year's Wish
by Michelle Major, the first book in
The Fortunes of Texas: The Hotel Fortune!

"I didn't fall," she announced with a wide smile as he
returned the crutches.

"You did great." He looked at her with a huge smile.

"That was silly," she said as they started down the walk
toward his car. "Maneuvering down a few steps isn't a
big deal, but this is the farthest I've gone on my own
since the accident. If my parents had their way, they'd
encase me in Bubble Wrap for the rest of my life to make
sure I stayed safe."

"It's an understandable sentiment from people who
care about you."

"But not what I want."

He opened the car door for her, and she gave him the
crutches to stow in the back seat. The whole process

was slow and awkward. By the time Grace was buckled in next to Wiley, sweat dripped between her shoulder blades, and she felt like she'd run a marathon. How could less than a week of inactivity make her feel like such an invalid?

As if sensing her frustration, Wiley placed a gentle hand on her arm. "You've been through a lot, Grace. Your ankle and the cast are the biggest outward signs of the accident, but you fell from the second story."

She offered a wan smile. "I have the bruises to prove it."

"Give yourself a bit of…well, grace."

"I never thought of attorneys as naturally comforting people," she admitted. "But you're good at giving support."

"It's a hidden skill." He released her hand and pulled away from the curb. "We lawyers don't like to let anyone know about our human side. It ruins the reputation of being coldhearted, and then people aren't afraid of us."

"You're the opposite of scary."

"Where are we headed?" he asked when he got to the stop sign at the end of the block.

"The highway," she said without hesitation. "As much as I love Rambling Rose, I need a break. Let's get out of this town, Wiley."

Don't miss
Her Texas New Year's Wish *by Michelle Major,*
available January 2021 wherever
Harlequin Special Edition books and ebooks are sold.

Harlequin.com

Love Harlequin romance?

DISCOVER.

Be the first to find out about promotions,
news and exclusive content!

Facebook.com/HarlequinBooks

Twitter.com/HarlequinBooks

Instagram.com/HarlequinBooks

Pinterest.com/HarlequinBooks

ReaderService.com

EXPLORE.

Sign up for the Harlequin e-newsletter and
download a free book from any series at
TryHarlequin.com

CONNECT.

Join our Harlequin community to
share your thoughts and connect
with other romance readers!
Facebook.com/groups/HarlequinConnection

Heartfelt or suspenseful, inspiring or passionate, Harlequin has your happily-ever-after.

With new books published every month, you are sure to find the satisfying escape you know you deserve.

HNEWS2020